Unmentionable

By Thomas Russel Cummings

Ch. 1 The Valley

People thought they imagined I existed. I've come to a different understanding of what my thoughts mean. Together, as a group or as an individual flesh out what I mean; agree or disagree on the truth. Thoughts begin to stir inside my mind. So much effort it has taken me to overcome a thoughtless existence, where I could not see beneath the surface of my identity like a murky pool. These thoughts provide me with hope that I can believe in myself once more. Emotion flows over me that I haven't felt in years like ice breaking up in a river after a long cold winter, revealing a strong current underneath. Along with the satisfaction I feel at my long-forgotten ability to think comes a painful ache due to the years it took me to reach this point, the years spent struggling.

I have a lucid dream. I often have dreams like this but this dream is different. The dream resonates with me. The river undulates and babbles as my eye follows its course to the next bend in the canyon. I hear a waterfall, but I do not trust my ears. There is a tree that has been upturned over the river. What upturned this tree? Pondering this conundrum, I examine the teeth marks on the trunk. It must have been a beaver. Exhausted by this line of thought I sit on the tree with my feet in the water. The current tickles my toes. An eagle soars not so majestically in the sky. I think that it noticed my gaze for it began to swoop and soar searching predatorily for prey. Laughing, I become disinterested in the eagle's theatrics as I see the mice in the valley turn to attention. Nearly forgetting the pleasant sensation of the cool river trying to push my feet towards the waterfall, I jerk my head downwards. The water is dark, but transparent. The strings of water between my toes bend with the wiggling of my feet amplifying the sound of water as melodiously as a guitar. Upriver a bear emerges from the forest to fish. I think to himself bears are very territorial of fishing space; I am glad that I am downwind, which gives me a moment before the bear notices my intrusion. The moment is gone by the time my thought is finished. Our eyes lock and I pretend to be dead. The bear doesn't have any delusions of grandeur; he doesn't believe his gaze has the power to kill. The bear approaches, while I halfheartedly do the Deadman's float. I say to himself,

"Screw this. Let's see if my crawl can get me out of this jam."

I am off in a flash. My eyes do not pay attention to the transparent dark water, the murky riverbed, the school of fish swimming beneath my shadow or the sound of a waterfall approaching, but focus on the bear I cannot see at my heels. My ears can only hear my heart, fueled by adrenaline, pumping a million miles per hour. My hands run out of water to cup. Feeling like Wily Coyote, I am caught in midair. Behind me the bear is laughing way up river, not giving chase. The drop is enormous. I think there is no way

I will survive. The wind bites at my face. My mouth opens, but no last words come out, only an unintelligible guttural babble. My body hits the water in a jumble. The water pushes me down to the depths of hell, as I am too beaten up to struggle against the unrelenting force.

I come to consciousness in mid-blink. I inhale so deep. Standing up in shallow water, I drop to my knees and thank God for sparing my life. I walk out of the water and take stock of my condition. Linear gashes bleed from my back. It is night. The light of the stars and moon make the shadows of the daytime move with new life. The wind blows and the trees cackle, the leaves sputter and the helicopter seeds spin to the ground. Owls hoot, crickets chirp, and my ears ring, as I try to unclog them. I am on an island and the river is too wide for me to swim across in my condition. Curling up into a ball, I fall asleep on the accommodating ground.

The sound of three men awakens me. I keep my eyes closed and listens to three voices: "I think we should take him to Monrovia to work in diamond mines." An authoritative voice interjects, "we will decide to bring him to Monrovia, or to Latvia later, now Achmetha bind his legs and Golgotha get his hands." I move with the quickness of a cheetah. My adrenaline filled heart contracts violently, as my muscles all move at once. I throw sand in Golgotha's eyes, and kick Achmetha. I run and explode into the water. A voice chases after me, calling "you can run but you cannot hide." The current is strong. The men give chase in a motor boat; I go under water. A multitude of bullets swim by like beams of light. One bullet hits my forearm; I cannot see the blood, for the water is too dark. With strength previously unknown, I swim underwater for ten more yards and reach the shore. Achmetha stands on the shore in front of me. I wipe the goofy grin off Achmetha's face with a tremendous right hook. Golgotha pistol whips me from behind. The sound of the hit was more vicious than the actual blow. My body crumples to the ground.

My mind is feverish. I black out and regain half-consciousness intermittently. I am half awake. I am still in the accursed valley moving along in a jeep. It is so dark in the daytime; a large mountain blocks the sun and I am immersed in shadow. Only Golgotha and Achmetha are in the jeep, and I wonder where the third man went. His voice still shrills in my head, "you can run, but you cannot hide." I fight the fear that there is no hope. The jeep stops in a green pasture. Achmetha states, "We need to get you cleaned up and fed before we try to sell you." I hide a smile as Achmetha unbinds my arms and attends my wound, while Golgotha prepares a table of food.

I am invigorated, my wounds throb has died down and my stomach is full. Golgotha tries to tie my hands back together. I grab the rope, race under Golgotha's legs, and rap the rope around his neck from behind. Golgotha flips me over his head; I use this momentum to kick Achmetha in the face. Achmetha goes down and Golgotha is rabid. Golgotha's gun is in the jeep, so he unsheathes a knife and approaches. Golgotha steps on the table cloth, which has fallen to the ground in the fray. I grab the cloth and pull, Golgotha goes to the ground and loses his knife. I jump on top of Golgotha and beat him senseless.

I am driving along in the jeep. The fields are green and the water is quiet. My soul is resting after the melee. The path I take is meandering and the land around it is perilous, but I am vigilant. The path will lead me out of the valley and to my dwelling.

I wake up wondering whether or not last night was real or not. At one point in the night I remember waking up and someone is holding a crack pipe to my mouth. Another person holds my nose and I inhale the crack smoke and then I pass back out again. Questions pound through my head. Was that real? Am I crazy? Was it just a dream? I go downstairs and pour myself some Cheerios.

I'm nineteen and living at home after taking a medical leave of absence from a small liberal arts school down south. I'm seeing a psychiatrist and am on a lot of medicine including sleeping medicine. I contemplate,

"Maybe I'm just having a bad reaction to the medicine."

Then it begins. My left eye starts blinking uncontrollably. Every time I blink I "hear" someone talking in my head.

The voice says, "Hello Denis."

As the realization that I am experiencing something so beyond any horrible fate I could have imagined just a short time ago, a few thoughts race through my head at all at once. These voices aren't real. They don't know who I am. If I come at this from my normal perspective, then I will either die or be in a strait jacket for the rest of my life. In other words, the only thing I can hope for is to survive. I can't hope to be happy, satisfied or fulfilled. I just want to be "normal" again. I think to myself that I can't possibly get through this, so I might as well be a man about it and accept what was happening to me.

The voice says, "I want you to go to the apartment complex that you drive by every day."

Without a second thought I get dressed, get into my car and drive five minutes to the apartment building that I knew the voice was talking about. I walk to a random door. The voice says, "knock on the door."

I think about it and muster the courage to knock on the door. No one answers. I get back into my car and drive home. I get back into bed. It feels as though my eyes are pried open and I can't shut them.

The voice tells me, "We're the Crips."

I don't say anything back.

The voice says, "That isn't going to work."

I take the voice for its word, knowing that I probably can't get away with saying nothing and say back, "Fuck you."

The voice says, "We're the Crips and we are going to boot you. But before that we're going to figure out why you are the way you are. We're going to make you tell us your life story."

I think to myself I'm fucked anyways why not tell the Crips in my head my life story, there's not much I can do about my situation anyway; I have no power over the current state of affairs. I begin with one of my first memories.

I tell the voices in my head about what must have been my second or third birthday. I am in my back yard with a few playmates. While my friends sit in the sand box, I listen to music from a kid's cassette deck with headphones on. I am listening to a Beach Boys song on a radio and look up into the Beach trees in my back yard. They are about two hundred feet high, it is fall and the wind is blowing. I dance to the song and look up at the leaves falling from the gargantuan trees. I remember feeling like I was cool.

The voice says, "The Beach Boys? What, did you grow up in the Brady Bunch or some bullshit? You must have been a little shit as a kid. Your mother should have swallowed you."

I think to myself that I shouldn't contemplate what is going on. I shouldn't try to understand. I shouldn't treat these voices like they were real. I tell them memory after memory, because I feel that if I give a fuck about what is going on, then I would feed the voices energy. Yet at the same time I am becoming livid, thinking to myself, I refuse to go out like this.

I'm in pre-school at the Church of the Savior. It is playtime in the yard of the Church. Like many days my friend Joey and I feel rambunctious and abscond from the rest of the preschoolers. Joey and I head straight for the tall pine tree, that we weren't supposed to climb, midway between the road and the Church on the back walk. I feel brave that particular day, point into the branches of the tree and say to Joey,

"Let's climb to the top!"

Joey says, "Yay! Let's go to the top!"

We begin the climb. Joey and I don't say much to one another as we use our small limbs to assiduously maneuver from branch to branch. We reach about midway up the tree and look down, and despite the dizzying height, my adrenaline fuels my desire to go higher up. I yell and laugh,

"Higher! Higher! Up to the Top!"

Joey giggles and says, "Yay! Let's go to the top!"

We climb inexorably onwards, higher and higher. I get to a point where as I reach for the next branch I can feel that it can't hold my weight. I look up and see Joey a few branches higher. I yell,

"We better stop!"

Joey looks down at me then looks down at the ground. His face turns to horror as he sees the distance between us and the Earth. He starts to cry. I say,

"Its ok Joey lets climb down."

He says, "No, I can't, we're too far up!"

As I try to convince Joey to come down playtime ends and I hear the whistle blow. A few minutes later I see Ms. Ivan standing at the bottom of the tree. She yells,

"Denis, Joey what are you doing climbing up there? You know you aren't supposed to climb the tree!"

I say, "I'm sorry. Joey's afraid. He can't come down."

Joey wails, "Too far up!"

Ms. Ivan says, "Denis! You've got to tell Joey to come down!"

I think rapidly. I muster all of the three-year-old power of persuasion I can employ and say,

"Joey lets go down, you are braver than me! You climbed higher up! Come down the branches are strong!"

Joey seems to regain some of his composure and finally starts climbing down.

I finish the memory and the voice inside my head says,

"Fuck your life sucka. You were crazy back then, too weren't you? You probably wanted your friend Joey to climb higher than you and fall off the tree."

I think to myself that if I'm going to survive this I have to be as calm as possible, as cold as ice.

I say, "Nah man, I just wanted to climb the tree and Joey was my boy. I was just a normal kid."

The voice says, "What else do you remember?"

I can't help but to wonder to myself about what is happening to me. I think to myself that we all think about different things throughout our lives. But what if thoughts transcended life? I mean, could it be possible that in some twist of fate we are all slaves to our thoughts? I'm not saying that there's a collective conscious, but that however improbable, it could be the case that thinking exists beyond our minds. That our life isn't determined by chance, or fate even, but by decisions our thoughts make that are beyond our comprehension. I think that it is possible that we exist to serve our thoughts, which exist on another level than who we are.

A part of me is insane, I accept that. But a part of me isn't. The core of who I am knows that this isn't real, but that I have to fight anyways to survive. The part of me that thinks clearly knows how fucked I am. So, I continue my life story.

I'm three years old, at my parents' friends' lake house. My parents start up the grill after my Mom changes me into swim trunks. My Mom says,

"I'm going to go inside for a minute, don't go past your waist in the water while I'm not here."

I play in the shallow water of the lake. I notice the minnows swimming underneath the surface. A motor boat speeds through the center of the lake. I look at the clouds. The shapes of clouds dominate the skyline. The edges of the clouds resemble frayed edges of a piece of paper. The clouds are an avalanche in slow-motion. The pillars of white fluff invade any sense of symmetry a blue sky could offer. Wisps of white billows race underneath the larger clouds. Light cascades from recesses. The dark underbellies of the cumulous clouds contrast sharply with the top of the clouds, which emit whiteness so bright it hurts the eyes. These clouds cast ominous shadows on unsuspecting people below, who continue their pursuits as if the sun is shining squarely in their faces. In a change of fortunes, the blue sky turns into negative space, as clouds devour the last bits of sky like hungry dogs. Through evaporated water, nature reveals its unrelenting force.

good

I think about how the adults don't let me do what I want. I think,

"I don't want to listen to Mom."

I look around the shore. The adults are preoccupied. I see my brother playing with his toy cars near the lake. I stare into the lake and splash the water. I think to myself,

"why not go in further?"

I do not know how to swim, but this doesn't deter me. I am curious as to what it feels like submerge myself into water where my feet can't touch the ground. I go in too deeper and my feet get tangled in the weeds of the lake. I panic and go under, franticly waving my arms. The next thing I know My brother Andrew is pulling me from the lake.

My parents and their friends rush over and give Andrew and me a hug. My Mom, crying says to Andrew,

"You saved Denis from drowning!"

The voices say, "You went in too deep, because you wanted to commit suicide, right? You were trying to off yourself."

I say, "Nah, I was just a child. I should have listened to the adults who told me not to go in too deep, but I didn't."

The voice says, "Maybe you'd be better off if Andrew didn't save you. Next story."

It is a spring morning. The entire third grade class is on the recess field. Our play is regulated to three fourths of the field. Temporary classrooms are built in one area to house the kids displaced by the asbestos being removed from the school. The recess field is caged in by a chain link fence that seems thirty feet tall. All the kids are restless, for the year at school is coming to an end. I am playing on the basketball court when I look across the field to see that my friend Hank is being chased by ten kids. Without much hesitation I run across the field and through the mass of taunting children to Hank's side.

Warren, the instigator of the merciless abuse, bellows out a laugh, "Look at these two jerks."

Hank, with newfound vigor, shouts back, "You're an ass Warren."

The other kids shout over one another to get their licks in. They all have a malicious glint in their eyes. I see that my supposed friends, Tim, Larry, and Johnathan are in the group. They all shout louder than the rest, galled that I had thrown my lot with Hank. We are all in the middle of the field with the assailants in a semi-circle around Hank and me. The verbal melee gruelingly rages on non-stop for ten minutes. I say a few things that shut some kids up. Then recess ends.

Some of the kids shouting at me and Hank are my friends. As children, we fought, rustled, tumbled, argued, misbehaved and roughhoused with each other. In the end we always made up, it wasn't serious. But this instance is serious. Basically, half of our class is kicking Hank when he's down. I can't watch this massacring of pride without taking it seriously.

I tell the voices another story about Hank. Later in the third grade, Tim, Larry and I walk leisurely through the teacher's parking lot and talk about what we are doing during the summer. I notice Tim's eyes dilate sharply. He points to Hank, twenty yards ahead, on the sidewalk running perpendicular to the parking lot and says, "Lets beat him up." Larry seconds the motion quickly. I am more hesitant. "Why do we always have to pick on Hank? I don't want to do it." Tim cajoles, "Don't be a wimp. It will be fun." I am convinced by this simple argument. We all sneak up behind him. I push him to the ground and pin his arms down with my knees. Tim and Larry give two or three punches to the stomach each. I cannot bear to look Hank in the eyes. In the extremely fast moment this happens, I realize that I have plans to go over to Hank's house later that day.

On the walk home, I rack my brain for an excuse to not go to Hank's house. I try to tell my mom that I'm sick, but she doesn't believe me. For lack of ideas, I'm driven over to Hank's house. In the car, I sweat like felon being brought to jail. I knock on the door; the footsteps pound in my head like a wrecking ball. Hank's mom answers the door and beckons me inside. She sits me down and says,

"Friends ought never to do what you just did. You shouldn't follow the crowd and do things that will hurt your friend like that."

"I'm very sorry Mrs. Carpenter. It will never happen again."

"Alright, you can go play now."

I see Hank peeping around the corner, and run over to him. We hang out the rest of the day like nothing happened.

The voice says in my head, "You was a fuckboy and your friend Hank was a fuckboy. Alright, I'm starting to get a picture of you as a kid, fuckboy."

Rage is building up in me, not so much at my situation, which is beyond fixing, but at these voices. I don't deserve this; it became clear to me that this is a living nightmare. Reality is slipping away from me and even though a part of me remains sane, the insane part of myself seems to be taking control.

I tell the voices about the first time I went skiing. I am three or four years old. My Dad puts on the ski boots. I tell my Dad,

"The boots feel wrong. Maybe it goes the other way?"

My Dad laughs and says,

"This is the way they go on silly! Let's put on the skis now!"

I say, "The boots feel wrong. They hurt."

My Dad gets angry and says, "I put them on right. Stop being fussy!"

The skis snap onto the boots. My Dad walks down the small slope and joins my Mom and my brother at the bottom. Dad says,

"Ok Denis, point the skis down the hill and ski down now!"

My heart pounds in anticipation at my first foray into skiing. I point the skis down the slope and laugh as I start to slide down. But my legs keep on spreading apart. I do a split and fall over.

My Dad says, "It's okay Denis. Lets' try again."

He picks me up and brings me back to the top of the hill. But I know the boots are on wrong because they hurt. I say, "The boots are on the wrong feet. My foot hurts."

Dad says, "No they aren't let's try this again."

He walks to the bottom of the hill and says,

"Okay Denis ski down now!"

I try again. To my dismay I do a split again and fall over.

My Dad tries to get me to ski down the hill over and over again but I can't. The boots are on the wrong feet.

Dad becomes livid that I can't ski. Eventually he gives up and says to Mom,

"Let's go home! Denis can't ski."

I am crying, at my Dads anger, but mostly because my feet hurt. My Dad takes off the boots and I see huge welts on my feet.

Several days pass with the voices dissecting my mind, draining me of my memories, feeding on my life like a parasite. I haven't slept in three days, I can barely eat anything and I call out of work. The voices probe, insult and disrespect me. There is nothing I can do but continue with my story.

I'm nine years old, at my family's lake house in Wisconsin and playing in back of the cabin with Andrew. Andrew says, "Jesus, do you see that bear?"

I look up but I don't see a bear where he's pointing.

I say, "No I don't see a bear, quit messing around."

Andrew says, "I'm not kidding, I see a bear."

I look again, still not seeing the bear. But Andrew apparently believes that there is a bear nearby, I decide to take his word for it.

I say, "let's play dead and if there's a bear it might go away. We play dead for about five or ten minutes then run back into the cabin and tell our parents what just happened. Our parents tell us that we imagined the bear, but Andrew is not so sure.

The voices say, "You saw the bear, didn't you? It wasn't there but you imagined it like your parents said, am I right? You were seeing things even back then."

I say, "I guess I was crazy for not being crazy."

In fourth grade I take an IQ test, as my parents decide to put me in private school. The woman giving me the test says,

"From here on out everything I say is part of the test."

I say, "Ok"

She starts giving me the test. I had taken tests before and done well. I am proud by now of my test taking ability. I even tested into the accelerated class at public school third grade. As the woman asks the questions I start giving answers. I realize that every question is connected to one another, and that how I answer one question will affect my score on all the others. So, I apply this knowledge and feel a bit giddy at how well I think doing. I start thinking that the reason that I am unhappy is that I am not being taught the way I should, and that if I get a good grade on this test I can go to a school that would teach me what I needed to learn. The woman stops the timer and says,

"Don't answer the questions like that."

I'm confused but say, "OK"

Then I remember what the woman said in the beginning of the test, that "From here on out everything I say is part of the test." So, I continue answer the questions as before, happy at how I could answer the questions the way I wanted to again. The test administrator stops the timer once again and says with a grimace,

"Why are you still answer the questions like before? I told you to stop."

I say, "You said at the beginning of the test that 'From here on out everything I say is part of the test.'"

The woman says, "This is not a part of the test. If you continue to take the test the way you are I will railroad you. You understand?"

I say meekly, "Yes."

I think that at this point in the test it doesn't matter what answers I give and pick at random. We go into the next room where my Mom is waiting and the woman says, "Denis has a 115 IQ. Not as smart as his brother who's 120 but good enough."

The voices say, "So, you got into the private school good for you. You think you are smarter than everyone? Look where you're at now."

I say, "I guess being smart doesn't predicate one from being booted."

I tell the voices about how I would get dizzy for no apparent reason. One day, in sixth grade, I enter my house returning from school, when suddenly the world starts spinning. I close my eyes and hope it will pass, but I can't compose myself and fall over. My Mom witnesses my fall and rushes over to me saying,

"Denis, are you okay? Why did you fall over?"

Freaked out I say, "I don't know. Everything started spinning."

We go to the hospital that night. After getting an EKG, the doctor informs me that I have a bad case of vertigo. My parents are worried sick and I miss a few days of school. I fall over again and again. I can't really leave my house. I have to walk with a cane. I end up missing most of sixth grade. I do schoolwork from home most of the year. Eventually, I get better and return to school.

The voice laughs then says, "You were faking vertigo, weren't you cocksucker. You did it to get attention, am I right?"

I say, "Nah homie that shit was bug. I really had vertigo"

It's April, I'm eleven years old and at my grandparent's cabin in Wisconsin. Andrew and I are walking on the frozen lake. It's bitter cold that day; as we traverse the frozen water we converse. Andrew says,

"When we get older, let's go into business with one another, we could be brother directors, like the Cohen brothers."

I consider about his proposal, then remember how Andrew would tease me. Not sure whether or not this was another jab at my ego I say,

"I don't know; I don't know if we would work well together as adults."

Andrew says, "Why not? Wouldn't it be cool if we were partners?"

I start to hear flowing water.

I say, "Do you hear that? It sounds like the lake isn't completely frozen over."

Andrew says, "Yeah I hear that. But it's still winter. The lake must be frozen over. Why don't you want to be my partner as adults?"

I say, "I definitely hear water. This lake isn't frozen over completely I can tell."

Andrew says, "Fine! I don't think it matters, but let's walk on the side of the lake."

A few hundred yards later in our walk, we notice unfrozen water flowing.

The voices say, "Could it be that you are misremembering the story? Maybe Andrew thought the lake wasn't frozen also and you're making it out like you're some sort of hero? You were greazy even back then."

I tell the voices about the incident with my brother in the hotel room. We are in a suite with my parents next door. I'm twelve years old. I wake up from a nightmare.

My brother Andrew asks, "You alright Denis?"

I say half asleep, "Yeah, I just had a nightmare."

Andrew says, "You have nightmares a lot, don't you? I never have nightmares. Maybe there's something wrong with you."

I say, "Everyone has nightmares, don't they?"

Andrew says, "I don't. Maybe there is something seriously wrong with you. What if your life becomes a nightmare?"

I say, "Shut up."

He says, "It could happen to you, where everything in real life is a nightmare."

I say, "I used to have horrible nightmares as a little kid, but they went away as I got older. All I had to do was dream that I had a clicker and that I could change the channel if I started to have a nightmare and they went away."

Andrew says, "Well the clicker isn't working anymore, and it's possible that your life will be like the nightmares."

For some reason this completely mindfucks me. I begin to wonder if this is possible. I start crying inconsolably. Andrew tries to get my mom, but my dad says that I'm too old to be afraid of nightmares. I spend the rest of the night crying.

The voice says, "Next memory bitch."

I am in eighth grade and my Mom picks me up from a friend's house. She prepares me for some bad news. Mom says,

"Denis, I know you had your heart set on going to Thatcher, Yates and Whittaker, but you got put on the waiting list."

Before I can put on a brave face and tell Mom that I don't care, I burst into tears. A few months later, after resigning myself to go to Lake High, another private school, to my joy I get in to TY&W.

I'm fourteen years old and at a camping orientation for freshman at TY& W. It is miserable. There is a tropical storm that hits during the orientation. We are supposed to be getting in touch with nature, and therefore have to start camp fires to cook food with just matches and we dig our own latrines. We sleep in tents throughout most of the storm. We bond as a group.

When academic year starts I look forward to doing the work and proving myself to my peers and teachers. A few days into the week I am walking back to the freshman common area when I hear crying. I peer into the lounge and about half of the small class is huddled around in small groups hugging and sobbing. I ask someone,

"What's going on?"

They say, "Dillon committed suicide last night."

I say, "Holy shit! How did he do it?"

They say, "I think he hung himself."

I am in shock. The moment is surreal. Most of my class are in histrionics and I feel pretty numb. The funeral is in a couple of days. I see my friend from middle school. He asks,

"Are you going to go to the funeral?"

I say, "I don't think so. This is overwhelming but I didn't really get to know Dillon. I don't know."

Myself and two other students decide not to go to the funeral.

The voices say, "Why didn't you go to the funeral? I guess you were too busy feeling yourself."

I say, "It seemed to me that many of the students in my class weren't as traumatized as they were letting on, and just wanted to get out of work. However, some are truly devastated and my heart goes out to those who really knew the student who killed himself."

The voice says, "Like I said you were too busy feeling yourself. Next memory."

It's the fifth day of not sleeping and the voices seem to be getting stronger as I get weaker. I just wanted to sleep, I just wanted to eat, I just wanted to cry, but I couldn't do any of those things so I move on to the next memory.

Later in my freshman year, my friends, Travis, Henry, George and I are waiting around for a ride to my house on a Friday. We have about an hour to kill. It's after sports practice so we are all tired and not thinking clearly. Travis says,

"I'm so fucking hungry. Is the cafeteria open?"

I say, "No its Friday, it closed about an hour ago."

The rest of us relate and wonder where we could get some food. One of my friends suggest that we go to the kitchen of the neighboring school and take some food. I naively ask,

"Does the other school care if we take food from their kitchen?"

Henry says, "Nah, I don't think so. I used to go there and my brother goes there so they'll probably be cool with us."

We walk behind the gym over to the kitchen of the adjacent school. The kitchen is empty and we help ourselves to some peanut butter and bread. As we walk back to TT & W we hear someone yell,

"Hey, you kids! Come back here!"

I turn around and see a woman about fifty yards behind us yelling. I say to my friends,

"Don't run! If we run then they'll know that we knew we were doing something wrong. Let's just act like we didn't hear her."

So, we deliberately walk back to the front of our school's gym and start eating our bounty. As we munch on the peanut butter and bread the gym supervisor approaches us. He says,

"You must be the kids that are in trouble. Come with me."

We walk with the supervisor back to his office. He has us sign our names. Myself, Travis and George sign our real names, but I notice that Henry signs "Joe Schmoe."

I go to school the next day and wait for the other shoe to drop. A teacher approaches me in the Freshman lounge and asks,

"Were you caught taking food from the school next door? Who was the fourth student with you?"

I say, "Yes I was and Henry was the fourth student."

She leaves, but doesn't believe me for some reason about Henry. After much confusion about the Joe Schmoe moniker, we are all brought in front of the disciplinary council, composed of both students and teachers. The head of the disciplinary council, Mr. Goddard, opens the hearing by saying,

"This is a very serious offence, stealing food from the Hall School, even though you don't seem to be aware of the seriousness of your actions. Not only did you show disrespect to our neighbor, you stole from them on top of that. What do you have to say in your defense?"

I say, "We are very sorry for causing so much trouble, but we thought that it was ok to take food from the Hall School. Henry used to be a student there and his brother attends the Hall School now."

Mr. Goddard says,

"All that is irrelevant. You weren't at the Hall school for any particular purpose, like picking up Henry's brother, you were there solely with the intent of stealing food. So, you didn't know it was wrong to steal food from the school next door? Travis, what would you do if someone broke into your house and stole bread from your kitchen? You'd be upset I imagine and would maybe call the police, right?"

Travis says, "With all due respect, I don't think that example is relevant to this situation. We didn't know that we were stealing from the kitchen. I guess if someone broke into my house and stole bread, I'd be empathetic. I'd worry if the man was homeless or hungry and I wouldn't call the police."

This answer seems to make Mr. Goddard angry. He turns to me and asks,

"So, you didn't know you were doing anything wrong? Why then did you run away when poor Ms. Grassmore from the Hall School saw you with the stolen items?"

I say, "We didn't run away, we walked back to the gym. We didn't think Ms. Grassmore was yelling at us?"

Mr. Goddard scoffs and says,

"You didn't think that Ms. Grassmore was yelling at you, when you had just stolen bread from their kitchen. The food they leave out is for Hall School students only! You must have known that when you stole the food! Now Denis, did you walk or did you run away from Ms. Grassmore? She says that you ran."

I think for a moment and say, "We walked."

After over two hours of this grilling the disciplinary hearing ends. Travis, George and I get one day suspension and Henry winds up with two days.

The voice says, "You ratted son. You snitched on your friend who wrote down the phony name. Fucking snake."

I say, "No honor amongst thieves, right?"

The voice says, "Next memory."

It's my sophomore year and I hear about an abandoned mental institution that is supposed to be haunted. Apparently, the patients had been subject to inhumane conditions and the government shut down the hospital, when the sadistic treatment came to light. This mental hospital was run before more modern medicine, which created a revolving door between the hospital and the home, was introduced into the mental health system. At that time, the insane had to be kept under lock and key. Anyways, three friends and I walk onto the grounds on the fourth of July. A guard approaches and asks, "what are you doing here."

My friend Amjid says, "We heard this place was haunted and we wanted to check it out."

The guard says, "That's cool. If I were you I would stay out of the underground tunnels though."

I say, "Thanks dude."

We continue our walk and arrive at a church. On the outside over the door spray painted are the words, "Forgive them Lord, they know not what they've done." We walk through the doors and the interior of the church is painted black and we see satanic graffiti scrawled across the walls. We decide to explore a bit in single file. I take the lead because I have the most balls. We walk up the stairs, progressively getting more freaked out. At the top of the stairs we hear a weird noise and jet out of the Church. It was so scary we don't have the nerve to go into any of the other buildings. We walk on the outside of the grounds, and watch the fireworks from a neighboring town then leave.

The voice says, "Next memory."

I'm sixteen years old, a junior in public high school. My brother recently graduated from high school but is having some issues. Andrew had been sleeping in the basement of late. I go down the stairs to the room in the basement. I knock on the door to see what Andrew is up to. Andrew answers the door and lets me in. The basement room had originally been all white without any windows, earning the nickname of the womb. However, in recent years Andrew and my friends had taken to writing and drawing on the walls. I say,

"What are you up to?"

Andrew says, "I'm about to take these shrooms. You want to try some?"

I had smoked my fair share of pot, but I had never done mushrooms before. I am intrigued. I say,

"Sure. Why not."

I take about an eighth of mushrooms. It's a school night and my parents are upstairs sleeping, but I didn't really know what I was getting into. The trip starts off great. Before I know it, I'm tripping hard and the graffiti and the drawings in the womb start to merge and move around on the wall to the sound of the jazz music. I say to Andrew,

40

"I never understood why people called a trip a trip before. It's like going on a journey. It's like going on a spiritual journey."

Andrew says, "Yeah it's pretty mind blowing, right?"

I say, "Are there other people like us? I mean are we special in that we understand things others don't?"

Andrew says, "Yeah maybe. I think your just tripping."

I say, "Holy shit! I've got to go to school in a few hours and I'm completely fucked up!"

I start getting anxious. I have school in a few hours but I'm hallucinating at this point. I think that I can't go to school and wonder how I can get out of going. Andrew goes upstairs into his room. I sit in the womb and try to put school out of my mind but can't. I start to feel claustrophobic. I go upstairs into the TV room. I look around the living room, and it appears as though a bulldozer had run over everything. It looks so real. I can't tell that I am hallucinating. I open the back door and look outside. I stare at the TV room in ruin and then contemplate running away outside. Andrew is suddenly at my side.

I say, "I did this didn't I?"

Andrew says, "why don't you go upstairs."

I take his advice as I have school in about an hour. I go to my room and try to fall asleep, all the while freaking out. My parents wake up and knock on my door.

Mom says, "Time to go to school."

I say, "I'm sick."

Mom says, "No, you aren't. Get ready for school."

I get up and start to take a shower. I panic. I pretend to fall down in the shower. When I get out of the shower I tell my Mom,

"I fell. I think I might be hurt. I can't go to school today."

Mom says, "I don't care if you were drinking all night with Andrew! You are going to school!"

The drive to school is nerve-racking. Mom drops me off and makes sure I go through the doors. As soon as she drives off I leave campus and take public transit back home.

The voice says, "You slipping son. Might have *you're* caught an L just then. You always been 7:30 huh?

I say, "It's a crazy world."

The voice says, "Next memory."

I tell the voices about how things change after that night. I used to be able to plow through a thousand-page book in a week just for fun. But, after that night I can't finish books I read outside of school for some reason. I get really into meditation. I start listening to underground hip-hop. I get into the habit of smoking lots of weed. I start smoking cigarettes. I graduate from high school and get into a pretty good college down south. The summer before I leave for college I quit smoking cigarettes and weed.

Ch.2 Grand Canyon

During the summer after graduating from High School, I decide to quit pot and cigarettes. Andrew and I hear about a hypnotist who works. The night before our appointment with the hypnotist, I chain-smoke. As I'm chain-smoking Andrew asks,

"You really are sucking them down. You think that's smart to do before you see the hypnotist?"

I say, "Hypnotism doesn't really work. It's pretty much BS. But if I am so addicted to cigarettes that I'm willing to try that, I really have to quit."

I have a premonition that my life wouldn't go in the direction I wanted it to if I continued to smoke weed and butts. We go to our appointment. The receptionist says, "Ok, everyone who goes in to see the guru has to throw out all their smoking paraphernalia." I throw away my lighter and cigarettes. We go in and the guru tells us about his life. He gives a lot of really good advice. He talks for about hour about his experience in the military and the testing he did relating to ESP. Then he asks us to see him individually a part from the group. I go in.

The guru says, "You're never going to quit cigarettes."

I say, "Then what am I doing here."

He says, "Close your eyes and imagine you're smoking a cigarette till the day you die."

I do this and he yells, "WAAAAH!"

I open my eyes and say, "That's it?"

He says, "That's it."

I leave the room. The voices say,

"The guru was right. You're never gonna quit. Why even try?"

I'm eighteen and leaving home for the first time to go to a small liberal arts school in Florida. I get to the school a few days early and find my dorm. I enter my dorm room and am greeted by my roommate, Trey. Trey says,

"Hey, you must be Denis. I'm Trey nice to meet you."

I introduce myself as well. We got to know each other on the phone a bit over the summer. I check out the dorm, which consists of two rooms separated by a door. The door to the hallway goes into the first room with the door to the second room being more secluded. I see that Trey had unpacked all his stuff in the more secluded room. I ask Trey,

"How early did you get here?"

He says, "I drove down about a week ago."

I say, "I guess you beat me to the punch."

Trey say, "I guess so."

The next night I am unpacking in my dorm when I hear a knock at the door. I open the door and am greeted by one of my classmates.

He says, "Hey, I'm Seth and I'm the RA for this floor. You're Denis, right?"

I say, "Yeah hey nice to meet you. I just got here last night."

Seth says, "Cool, cool! Are you get situated alright?"

I say, "Yeah, man. Thanks. Anything going on tonight?"

Seth says, "Yeah, definitely! We're having a fight club in the basement. You can get in on a fight if you want. No pressure."

I say, "Hmm that sounds kind of fun. Sure, I'll do that."

Seth says, "Cool. Your roommate agreed too. You two can have a fight!"

I say, "Word!"

Fight club is in about an hour. I sit in my dorm and listen music. I talk with my new roommate.

I say, "I'm not going to really fight. I don't want to take it seriously."

He says, "Neither do I."

I say, "I just want to have some fun. I think the whole idea is a little stupid but whatever."

Trey says, "Yeah definitely. Lets' just have fun."

I say, "Our fight is probably coming up. Let's go down."

We take the elevator down to the basement. Seth says,

"Everyone this is fight club. You know the first rule of fight club: you do not talk about fight club. Second rule of fight club: you do not talk about fight club. Third rule of fight club: you do not talk about fight club. Okay let's get this started."

Two classmates put on the boxing gloves. The gloves aren't regulation boxing gloves, but kid gloves with just enough protection so that you don't hurt your fists. About thirty or forty spectators from the dorm, shout and cheer to fighters on. Lincoln Park blasts from the stereo. The fight stops after about five minutes. It wasn't too brutal. But I'm getting a little anxious as I notice Trey getting hyped up watching the fighters. He's about my height 6'3", but he has about fifty pounds on me. The next fight starts. These two really go at it. One of the fighters stops the fight.

It's my turn to fight now. Seth asks me, "What do you want to listen to in the CD Player?"

I had brought down my Wu-Tang Forever CD. So, I say,

"Wu-Tang."

And put in the CD. As the rap starts to play Trey says,

"Hold on. I don't want to listen to that. Let's play Tremendous D."

I am a little upset but don't really care all that much so I say,

"OK."

The fight begins and I start throwing left hooks to the dome. I test him out a little. Then Trey starts throwing a few haymakers at me. I realize that this is a little more than I was ready for. The crowd starts getting into it. I have to start taking the fight a little more serious. One of the freshmen from my dorm starts coaching me, screams,

"go for the body-shots! Hit him in the gut!"

So, I take a shot at his ribs. I don't know my own strength. Trey throws down his guard and looks a bit woozy. In that moment I can smack him with a right hook and he'd see stars, but I restrain myself with all my might; I don't want to start a thing on the third night at school. Trey then tries to play it off like I ain't shit and he looks to his side and shrugs his shoulders. He regains his composure and then bull rushes and pummels me into a chair. At this point I'm not defending myself and people have to pull him off of me. I still don't want to take the fight serious so I stop it. The next night they ask me to do it again and I refuse. Trey fights some big Junior that night, and I don't remember who won.

The voices say, "You got your knot rocked kid. You didn't even stop it. Trey fucked you up, didn't he?"

I say, "I remember it differently, but I could have won that fight if I knew what I was getting into. "

The voices say, "He bitched you out bitch. You don't even know how to shoot the fizz. Next memory."

Walking across campus, a woman about 5"2 with shoulder length brown hair and blue eyes approaches me. With a charismatic grin she introduces herself in a southern accent. "Hey I'm Tiff, are you a freshman?"

I say, "Hey Tiff, I'm, Denis nice to meet you. Yeah, I'm a freshman. What year are you?"

Tiff says, "I'm a sophomore, where are you from?"

I say, "I'm from Boston. What's your major?"

Tiff says, "I'm a theatre major. Well, Denis, I will see you around campus."

It's a pretty innocuous meeting but she leaves an impression on me. I guess she felt the need to extend some of the southern hospitality that you hear about. About a month later I ask Tiff out on a date. I take Tiff to a production of Othello at a neighboring college. We are sitting in the second row. As we wait for the play to start I ask,

"What's your last name?"

She says, "O'Connor."

Tiff O'Connor asks me what my last name is, I say, "Rigs."

After the play we sit in her car. She asks,

"What did you think of the play?"

I say, "It was okay, but I couldn't really get into it. I felt like the actors weren't really getting into their roles."

She says, "I didn't like it either. We can say that we didn't like it, right?"

I say, "Sure, of course."

She drives us to a café a few miles away. I had started smoking again at this point. We make small talk at lunch, but the whole time I'm thinking of having a cigarette. Finally, she asks,

"Are you okay? You seem distracted?"

I say, "Yeah, I'm okay. Do you mind if I have a smoke?"

She says, "Go ahead."

After lunch she drives me back to campus. We pull up in front of the dorm. I say,

"I had a great time hanging out with you. We should do this again sometime!"

She says, "Yeah cool."

I try to kiss her but she turns her head and I kiss her on the cheek.

I'm pretty reticent about the date. The conversation we had plays over and over in my head. I get a call on my cell phone, but I let it go to voicemail. Later I check the voicemail and hear a woman's voice saying,

"I love you."

I call Tiff and leave a voicemail saying, "I love you more than words can say."

I get a text from her a little later saying,

"I had a good time at the play, but I think we should be just friends."

At the end of the second semester there is a party at Daytona Beach. I call Tiff and say,

"So, I assume you'll be at the beach party? Are you driving?"

She says, "Yeah I'll be there. I'm driving my Dad's Corvette."

I ask, "Can I get a ride?"

She says, "No, it only has two seats."

I say, "Please."

She says, "No, sorry. But I hope to see you there."

I say, "Alright."

I call up my friend Fred, who is a part of the Z-Clan fraternity and he agrees to give me a ride. We arrive in Daytona, I'm wearing cheap aviator sunglasses from a gas station, a swimming suit and my favorite Bob Marley T-Shirt. I see Tiff. We start talking about movies, about music and about life.

Tiff says, "Your pretty good at shooting the shit."

I say, "Thanks so are you." We walk out into the water together.

Tiff says, "I'm going skydiving in a few weeks do you want to go with me?"

I ask, "Why do you want to go skydiving? I don't think I want to go, I have a golf tournament that day."

Tiff says, "I guess I want to go skydiving mostly just to impress my friends."

We walk back out the water. I try to continue the conversation, but she talks to other people. In my feelings I get really drunk. I throw up on the beach. At sunset the party dies down and we head back to the car.

A few weeks later the day of the golf tournament arrives and as I'm walking across campus with my clubs I see Tiff. She's about to go skydiving and asks me, "You sure you don't want to come skydiving with us?"

It was probably just a nice gesture that she asked, I don't think she was expected me to say yes. But I think about it for a second and I say,

"Sure, I'll go."

I give my clubs to my friend and get in the car with Tiff. I'm pretty nervous, but the people in the car are acting like it's no big deal. One of the guys in the car asks me,

"Are you afraid?"

I say, "Hell yeah I'm afraid, it would be stupid not to

be."

We get to the airstrip and sign the consent forms. I

find out that we are diving in tandem. I say to the group, "We

have to jump out the plane with someone strapped to our

back? Lame." We have a few hours to kill before the jump. I

try to talk to Tiff but she is in a conversation with someone

else. Finally, it's time to board the plane. The plane takes

off. We make the ascent to ten thousand feet, which takes

about a half an hour. I'm in the front of the plane and Tiff is

in the back. The whole time I want to turn around and see

Tiff, but I restrain the urge. After a couple of people jump

it's my turn. The instructor strapped to my back says,

"when we first jump out you aren't going to know

what's going on. Just get in the position we talked about."

I say, "Ok I'm ready."

We jump out the plane and I focus on putting my feet and arms back. The initial free fall is an adrenaline rush beyond what I've experienced before. We free fall for about ten minutes. I see the horizon and the ocean glistening down below. I yell in exhilaration, then the shoot opens. Right before we land on the ground the instructor says,

"Since you're so tall you're going to have to be the one to stand up. When I tell you stand up."

I say "Yeah, Okay."

We land and the instructor says, "Stand up now!"

I try to stand up. We both duck walk about fifteen paces. The instructor yells,

"Stand up now!"

I stand up and we make the landing. I wait about a half an hour for the rest of our group to land. One classmate exclaims,

"That was incredible! Better than sex!"

We walk back to the car. Tiff says to two in our group,

"You both probably want to sit together. I know how you feel."

They say, "Thank you Tiff."

Tiff and I sit in the back seat. We drive back to campus. I walk Tiff back to her room give her a hug and say,

"We did it!"

The voice says, "You jumping out of planes and shit trying to get some strip? No wonder you don't get any."

I say, "I wanted to be Tiff's friend first and foremost."

The voice says, "Next memory moron."

The second semester rush starts at the different fraternities. Rush is when the different frats try to recruit pledges. I learn that one of the fraternities had just got back on campus after being kicked off. Apparently, maybe ten years ago, members of the local fraternity, called Z-Clan, had gotten into a violent incident with another fraternity, I'm not sure what over, but they got kicked off campus because of it. But the reformed frat wants to eschew its troubled past and start anew. I meet a lot of the frat brothers and they seemed low-key and mellow, which is right up my ally. However, their pitch to many of the other rush attendees is that if they all joined they could be the new it frat. I am not that down with this pitch, but the frat brothers are cool and I liked them so I want to join.

The second semester, I need two more credits, in order to officially be a sophomore next semester. I needed those credits so I could bring my car and be able to park on campus. Trey suggests that I work on one of the school plays and gives me a sheet to sign up. I sign up to work in the woodworking shop and give the sheet back to Trey to give to the professor. When I go and meet with the professor, he says,

"I'll let you work on the play, but why do you want to work in makeup?"

I say, "makeup? I signed up for the woodworking shop."

The professor shows me the signup sheet and my signature is next to the makeup slot. He asks,

"Is this your signature here?"

I look and say, "Yeah that's my signature, but I don't remember signing up for makeup. Are there any spots left in the shop?"

He says, "No, but if you want you can work in the makeup department."

I think about it and say, "Sure."

The play goes well, but the actors don't give me much work in makeup. Before the play, I spend a lot of time in the dressing room. During the plays, there's no work for me to do, so I end up falling asleep a few times on the couch backstage."

When the play is over, the actors throw a party. They bring us individually onto the stage and say a little speech about each person and how they contributed to the play. It's my turn and I walk from behind the curtain and onto the stage. The person in charge of the ritual grills me and says,

"What made you think it was ok to fall asleep during the play? Don't you think you could have been doing something rather than sleeping. Are you lazy or something?"

Thinking on my feet I say, "I was just resting my eyes. I'm not lazy, I was just visualizing doing makeup."

Some people laugh and the emcee goes on to the next person, not pressing the issue. At this time, we are to divide into a bunch of groups of five or six people. I try to join the group that Tiff is in, but Trey grabs me by the neck and yanks me into his group. Not wanting to ruin the festive mood I acquiesce and remain in this group. The groups leave and separate. My group is pretty much all dudes, and I'm stuck with Trey, so I don't have a good time. We spend a few hours doing different activities around campus. Afterwards we all reconvene into one big group and start drinking. I drink a lot, more than my limit, about a bottle of vodka. I find myself sitting on the steps outside the building with Tiff. We start kissing and making out. I'm really hammered, it occurs to profess my love to Tiff. I want to get away from the crowd so I can talk to her. I say,

"Let's go over to that bench and talk, there's something I need to tell you."

Tiff says, "Tell me here, why do you want to go to the bench."

We argue over going to the bench and finally, I throw up my hands, drunk and exasperated. I walk off giving her the peace sign. I see my friend Ben, start talking to him and we end up going to his friend, Mark's apartment. In the apartment we chill on the balcony for a bit, someone is puking their brains out in the bathroom, I barely notice.

I say, "I'm enamored by that girl Tiff. I hope I didn't make a fool out of myself tonight I'm pretty wasted."

We talk about the party. Suddenly the bathroom door opens and there's Tiff puking her brains out, with no pants on and a man helping her throw up. I think to myself,

"I'm way too drunk to deal with this situation, I'd better go back to my dorm room."

So, I make the five-minute walk back to my dorm. I walk near the lake that the campus is on, and lie down in the sand. I try to get back up and return to my bed but I'm too drunk to get up. I close my eyes and nearly pass out on the sand, but I get a second wind and am able to stumble back to my room.

I briefly see Tiff the next day. My friend, Anthony invites me to his dorm for pizza and Tiff is there. She asks me,

"What did you want to tell me last night?"

I'm hungover and uncomfortable so I say, "I was drunk I don't remember. I saw you after the party at Marks apartment though."

Tiff says, "Oh yeah, what was I doing?"

I say, "You were puking."

I make an excuse and leave.

The voices say, "Makeup? You perv, you thought you could get with all the actresses in the dressing room, huh?"

I say, "I don't remember signing up for that, at the time I thought someone might have forged my signature.

After my freshman year at college I go on a trip to Europe with my friends Thurman and Ben. We take a train to the Swiss Alps to go hiking. We exit the cable car enclave and jump up and down with excitement. The view of the surrounding mountains demands a moment of appreciation. Thurman shouts to us,

"How dope is this!"

We take pictures of one another with the snow-capped peaks in the background. Thurman stares at one of the peaks above him and says,

"We've got to get up there."

I say, "That's a thousand feet up."

Ben says, "Let's follow the trail."

A local in his car is doing maintenance, next to a sign. Thurman asks him,

"Will this take us to the top of that?" The local shakes his head and states,

"The mountain has too much snow to climb, you should go that way."

The three of us follow the man's advice until the next corner in the path. We come across a field that rolls up the mountain invitingly.

I say, "I really want to climb a bit higher, let's head up that field and off this path."

After some deliberation the group marches off the trail and up the mountain. Ben complains that his foot hurts. I am a little peeved by the statement, the mountain was asking for exploration in my estimation and hurt feet hampers this adventure.

Thurman declares, "You obviously can hike a little bit, just tell us when you want to turn back."

Joe and I make our way up the field while Ben lags behind a little. Joe turns to me, as we wait for Ben to catch up and says,

"On a scale of one to ten, if we get to the cloud line, how dangerous will this be.

I ask, "Ten being certain death?"

At Thurman's nod I continue, "Up by the peak that's a seven or an eight, here it's a two."

Thurman, Ben and I reach the end of the field a tangle of trees that lies in our path. we start to get dirty, climbing under and over the serpentine branches. Joe kicks lose a watermelon-sized rock that rolls down and hits Ben in the shin. Ben curses, but is fine.

Ben asks, "How much further are we going to go?"

I say, "As far as you can last, Thurman and I want to climb about an hour longer."

We continue climbing. We walk into a dried-out stream. The rocks and dirt are slippery. The snow starts to slosh around in our shoes. Thurman comments to me,

"This is sort of ridiculous doing this in our street clothes."

I say, "yeah but this is getting more and more cool the higher we get up."

Two hours into the hike, the peak seems attainable. However, in order to reach the top, we will have to trek through 200 yards of snow and climb up several inclines that are 45 degrees in angle. We come across a pile of stones. I say,

"I think this is here to mark where somebody died. This guy probably was winter climbing. This is much safer in the summer."

Thurman and I urge Ben to continue with them to the top.

Thurman says, "This gets doper and doper the higher we get."

We are pressed for time. We don't know when the last cable car that goes down the mountain departs. The group presses on. Thurman steels himself to the task at hand. He nearly slips and falls, he curses himself. Thurman is completely focused after a half an hour of arduous walking; we reach the end of the packed snow. Ben lags a little behind, falls down then picks himself back up again.

Thurman and I assess the situation.

Thurman asks, "This next part looks a bit ridiculous. Do you want to go on?"

I say, "This whole climb is ridiculous, let's do it."

Thurman and I start up the next incline. The angle is sharp. Before we reach the top, we decide to turn back as the climb becomes too difficult. We run at break neck speed and just make the last cable car down the mountain.

The voice says, "What else do you remember"

I tell the voices about the beginning of my sophomore year at college. I am able to have a car for the first time at school so I go on a road trip with my father from my home Boston to the school in Florida. We take turns driving. As we drive down 95 South an ominous sky looms in the distance. As we speed down the highway, the sky turns black and thunder rumbles balefully in all directions. The rain starts pouring, becoming an antediluvian torrent. Lightning strikes all around us. A windshield wiper from the

Volvo breaks in the Sisyphean effort of clearing rain from the windshield. We debate whether or not to stop. Dad says,

"We could try to drive through this or stop somewhere and hope for the storm to pass."

I say, "I think we should keep on going."

We drive for about a half an hour and finally the rain calms down. We drive past DC. I'm speeding in the fast lane about ten miles over the limit. I flash my high beams at the cars driving slower in the left lane to make them aware I want to pass. My father has his feet on the dash. I might have pressed the brakes a little late when a car in front of me slows down. My father presses his feet down against the windshield as if his foot is on the brake, which makes a crack in the glass. We stop at a motel to spend the night in Fredericksburg, Virginia. The next day we go to the car and my father says,

"You see all the oil underneath the car?"

I look and see an oil spot. I say,

"Yeah, I see the oil spot, I'm not sure if that's from my car though. We might have just parked on it."

Dad says, "I don't think that's likely. I think that there's an oil leak in your car."

I say, "Ok, what should we do then?"

He says, "Let's take it to a repair shop and rent a car to go the rest of the way."

I agree and we take the car to an auto repair shop to have the mechanic check it out. We take a cab to Richmond and rent a car. We arrive at the off-campus house my sophomore year I'm renting with my freshman roommate, Trey. Trey had given me a key last semester. At around two in the morning my dad and I walk into the house. It's dark so I turn on the lights and see a strange man holding a baseball bat. A hectic exchange ensues.

Howard says, "Who the fuck are you?"

I say, "I'm Denis, who the fuck are you? Trey didn't tell me anyone else would be here."

Howard says, "Oh… You must be Trey's friend."

I say, "Yeah I'm renting a room here. Who the fuck are you?"

Howard says, "I'm the contractor. I'm staying here while I make repairs to the house."

The voices say, "Keep going."

The next day my Dad gets ready to leave for the airport. Right before I drove down there was a major hurricane in Florida. The house was half renovated and there was a tree in the pool. My Dad says,

"I hope you can focus on schoolwork while living here. The house looks like it needs a lot of work done."

I say, "Don't worry about me. Have a safe trip home. I love you."

Dad says, "I love you too."

Back at college, the day the different frats selected the pledges I had to choose between a frat that I thought the cool kids were a part of and Z-Clan. I choose Z-Clan, because the frat brothers seem like they have their shit together and are smart. After my choice, I meet the other new pledges, including Trey. Trey and a bunch of his friends had decided to join forces and join Z-Clan to try to become the next "it" frat. I realized I knew I made a mistake when I realized that out of the fifteen or so frat brothers I liked, twelve were seniors and only three would remain after my freshman year.

As the college braces for a second hurricane that season, I scramble to find a place to weather the storm.

I tell the voices about how I sort of went crazy over Tiffany. I start being morose and pining over her. I imagine her as a color. I imagine her as a vibrant blue, like in a Monet painting, like the color of her eyes. I see this blue in all aspects of his life. I see the blue in cars that drive past, in the sky and in other people. However, the color seems faded at times. I imagine other people seeing the blue color, as she shows her true self to them, but them not seeing it in the way that I do. This color emanates from Tiffany when I am with her, it is almost like a religious experience for me, and it blinds my eyes, fills my senses, and muddles my thoughts. It's uncanny the way my mind always comes back to Tiffany.

Along with this lovelorn mood I am in, I start becoming paranoid. About a week after I arrive at school for my third semester, I take a train ride back to Virginia to pick up my car. When I get there, I ask the mechanic what the problem is, or why there was an oil leak. He says that there is no problem with the car and that the oil hadn't leaked. As the semester progresses, this car situation irks me more and more. I begin to have delusions that my dad has been transporting drugs, without my knowledge and that the car breaking down was some sort of drop.

The voices say, "You fake loved some fake bitch. You that crazy huh."

I tell the voices, "I was crazy for not being crazy."

The voices say, "Next memory."

My sophomore year I spend a lot of time at the gym. I'm super in shape and play a lot of pick-up basketball. Even when there isn't a pick-up game happening I spend hours practicing my overall game. I've gained about forty pounds of muscle, since my lanky days in high school, now weighing about 220. I can even dunk the ball. I tell my roommate Trey that I can dunk, but he doesn't believe me.

Every Monday, there's a pick-up game that the professors play; Trey and I usually join. One Monday were playing the professor pickup game and I'm doing really well in the game. The opposing team tries to score in transition, I hustle back and get the rebound. I go on a fast-break, pounding the ball against the court planning on dunking the ball when I reach the basket. The only one left in my way is Trey around mid-court, as I dribble around him he doesn't even play defense, he just shoves me as hard as he can. The only thing I can do aside from fall on the court and break my neck is use the momentum from the shove to run. So, I run, frenziedly from mid-court to behind the basket, careening headlong into the cushioned wall. I get up and get in Trey's face, wanting to throw a punch but restraining myself.

The voices say, "You weren't going to dunk the ball. You can't dunk dipshit."

I say, "I could dunk the ball and was going to, but Trey was a son of a bitch."

I tell about how towards the end of the third semester at school where I have zero concentration and I'm becoming paranoid about my roommate Trey. I sit in the library and compose a love letter to Tiff. I know exactly what I want to say, but it takes me nearly four hours to handwrite about a page. I keep on making typos. Finally, I get a good copy down on paper.

Dear Tiff,

I don't want to rationalize how I feel. But I doubt myself all the time. I get afraid that my love for you is all in my head. I'm a virgin. I think that's partially because it's hard for me to pursue a girl I don't have real feelings for. Mostly, that's just who I am. I want to have sex, but I'd rather it be all or nothing with you. So, maybe the way I feel is biological since I'm so attracted to you and inexperienced with women. What scares me the most is thinking that nothing separates me from anyone else or that everybody is the same as everybody and what makes me think that I'm unique is arrogance and egoism. The last fear doesn't come specifically from you. However, in a major way you catalyze something else in me, courage. Courage that arises from this fear to make me try to become the man I want to be. The man I want you to see. Even though I would extend myself as much as I could the distance that separates us is as wide and as deep as the Grand Canyon. I'm asking you to take that jump and faith in me to meet you half-way. I would never let you down Tiff. It seems stupid to talk about love at age 19 and it probably is. But I try not to doubt myself.

Love,

Denis Rigs

I am writing this letter in the library of my old school, an emotional wreck, teetering on the edge, knowing that I shouldn't write it, or send it, but throwing caution to the wind. Creating many drafts but throwing them away knowing what I wanted to say but fighting with myself to write it down and struggling with my self-control. I send the letter.

After writing the letter I decide to take a medical leave of absence. I go through the process and return home from school. I start seeing a psychiatrist.

The voices say, "Don't stop now. We just getting started."

Ch. 3 Back at Home

Once back at home, my delusions get worse. I'm having racing thoughts and extreme paranoia. I go for a ride in my car. As I'm driving I notice a car that seems to be following me wherever I turn. So, I decide to drive through a dangerous part of town in Hyde Park. The car I think is following me turns in another direction and I am relieved.

About a week after I return home I chill with my friend Patrick. Most of my friends from High School are away at college, but not Patrick, he is not in college. Soon after we meet up at my house he says,

"I found an empty beer bottle in the middle of my room at my parent's house. I didn't leave it there. I asked my brother and he doesn't know where it came from. Do you have any idea how an empty beer bottle appeared in my room?"

I say, "I have no idea."

Patrick used to sell drugs and I assumed that this had something to do with that. That the beer bottle in his room was some sort of gang activity. In the past I wouldn't think that this had anything to do with me, but in my current state I am not so sure. I am trying to keep it together, but my mind is in overdrive, each thought coming as fast and as hard as a machine gun burst. I think,

"Could this have anything to do with me? Could I be unwittingly transporting drugs and some gangs are on to the operation that I'm involved in? What should I do? Should I go to the police?"

conspiracy?

I can't control the onslaught of thoughts that pound through my head. I am able to keep it together a little, a part of me is aware that I am not being rational. But my thoughts continue along this gangster line of thought and I can't think my way out of this loop.

Patrick says, "Oh well. Hey do you want to go for a ride with me to Cambridge? My Mom's birthday is in a few days and I want to get her a gift there."

I say,

"Sure."

We arrive at a small street in Cambridge and Patrick double parks his Honda Civic in front of a police station on a crosswalk.

Patrick asks me, "Do you want to go with me to the furniture store? I've got to buy a table for my mom. Or do you want to wait in the car."

I say, "I'll wait in the car."

I decide a second later to go with him. Before I exit the car, I lock the manual lock on my door and the driver door.

We go into a small bookshop. Patrick looks around and doesn't find what he wants. I am thinking to myself at this point,

"Why did Patrick double park his car in a crosswalk in front of the police station. Is this some sort of sting? Is Patrick going to get me arrested? What should I do?"

I decide to keep it cool. We go into three stores and spend about forty-five minutes away from the car. He finally buys a table. I wonder if there are drugs in the table and if I am going to be arrested. When we get back to his car, both doors and the trunk are locked, the hazard lights are on and his keys are in the car. Patrick curses at me,

"Why the fuck did you lock the doors? My extra set is at home and we are illegally parked in a crosswalk. I might have to go home and get the extra set."

In a quandary as what to do, Patrick walks up to a couple of cops on motorcycles, I assume to explain to them what's going on. Patrick walks back to the car.

Patrick says, "Shit! I think I might have to go home to get my extra set of keys."

The window on the driver side is cracked and I have long arms, so I tell Patrick, "Hey I think I might be able to reach in and get the lock."

I am able to get the car open and Patrick gives me a ride home. I sit in my house and think about what just happened, mind racing.

"Why didn't the police give us a ticket? We had parked illegally in the crosswalk for a long time and the police didn't even give a shit. Is Patrick working with the police? Could it be that in the table he bought was drugs and that I had foiled his plan to have the police arrest me by locking the car."

A few weeks later my paranoia and delusions cannot be contained. I confront my parents about what I believe to be true. We sit in the living room and I say,

"I know that you've been using me to mule drugs. You've been getting my friends to deal drugs and using me to deliver them."

My dad says, "No Denis, you've been having some mental issues and I think that you should talk to your doctor about this."

I press harder.

"The road trip down to Florida. The mechanic said that there wasn't an oil leak. Why did we leave the car in Fredericksburg? Was that some sort of drop?"

My Mom says, "You aren't making any sense. Have you been using drugs?"

My parent's denial makes me more convinced that my delusions are true. I leave my house and go to my friend Patrick's house down the street.

The next day I return home and find my mother,

I'm driving to the mental institution with my mother. Paranoia and delusions, racing thoughts and suicidal ideations permeate my thinking. It doesn't help that my mother asks me on the way to the hospital,

"Do you know what happened to the ounce of marijuana that your dad had in his office? It's missing."

I don't respond. Looking out the window it appears as though a gang of teenagers forty deep walk down the street. Inside I know that this has nothing to do with me, but I'm not thinking clearly. I think that this is the beef that people have with me. I wait in the waiting room, going through the process of checking myself into to the hospital. My father arrives. Right before I'm checked in he says to me,

"If you get through this you'll be able to get any job you want."

I don't know what to say. My mind, though not functioning correctly still is able to provide me with a little understanding. "This is a test of some sort?" I think to myself as I pass into the doors entering into the in-patient ward. The doctor shows me my room and introduces me to my roommate Jerome. Jerome is a black man from a dangerous part of Boston called Mattapan. He's wearing street clothing and lies in the bed lackadaisically. The doctor then explains to me that since I'm here voluntarily that I don't have to do anything I don't want to. A nurse with an intrusive glare tells me to fill out a piece of paper. I stare down and read the questionnaire. It asks,

"Who is the one person in the world who can calm you down? Do you want them to visit you?"

I approach the nurse and take better stock of her appearance. She has squinty eyes an aquiline nose and wavy blond hair probably in her forties.

I say, "you wrote this specifically for me and not for the other patients."

She says in a combative tone. "No, you're wrong we have a whole stack of these sheets on that desk."

I look over and see a large stack of sheets on a desk, but don't see what's written on them. I didn't ask for a closer look feeling that that would cross a line. So, I sit down to fill in the questionnaire. A different doctor than the one who showed me to my room approaches me.

He says, "Here, I am going to give you electric shock treatment, now take off your clothes."

I comply and strip down to my underwear. The doctor starts to place suction cups connected to a machine on my body. My mind is numb, the doctor puts the last suction cup onto my body and I stupidly sit on a table and wait for the doctor to shock me. Then I think to myself "I don't have to do this if I don't want to."

So, I begin to take off the suction cups. The doctor asks,

"What are you doing?"

I say, "They told me that I don't have to do anything I don't want to when I first got here."

The doctor, looking somewhat dejected, rolls the machine out of the room.

A male nurse with an accent from the Caribbean approaches me and says that I have to take a piss test. So, I go to the bathroom and urinate into a cup, then immediately poor its contents into the toilet and throw the cup into the trash. The nurse stares at me with anger and says in a firm voice,

"What are you doing, take that cup out of the trash and piss into it."

I stare back at him confused, "Do I have to?"

He answers, "Yes"

I comply with his request. The nurse and I begin talking after this incident. I say that I'm in trouble, my life is in shambles, he seems sympathetic. His name is Joakim he's from Haiti. I guess in an attempt to motivate me he tells me to run with him down the hallway, back and forth. He says in a thick Haitian accent,

"Don't run like that, run like a man."

After about an hour of running back and forth down the hallway he seems to be content with my body language. Next, a man who doesn't say who his position at the hospital starts to talk with me as I fill out yet another questionnaire. We talk for a long time he asks me about my experience at school. He talks with me as if he knows me; I'm disconcerted by this. It seems to me that this entire hospital is full of people, who are aware of my situation, and I'm not sure if they are here to help or to hurt me. I keep my suspicions to myself.

I lie down in bed. The hospital has people watching me because of the reason that I was there. I had been up all night before I was admitted considering committing suicide because of my unrequited love for Tiff. The night progresses, the people watching me on different shifts shuffle in and out of my room. Eventually I ask to go to the bathroom. As I exit the bathroom I slam the door open into an orderly's face knocking him down and I return to my room as if nothing happened. I hear people talking in the hallway,

"If he's this loud when he sleeps, he must be pretty fucking loud when he's awake."

The next day I see that the orderly from the night before has stiches on his head even though I hear nothing about the incident. They take me off of suicide watch, but I'm worried that I'll face retaliation for knocking out the orderly and giving him stiches, as I don't believe that he has forgotten what has happened. So, a few hours later I explain to a nurse that I'm still suicidal. They ask me how I'm thinking of killing myself in a hospital.

I say, "I was planning of breaking the glass of that window over there and slashing my wrists."

They seem to believe me and put me back on the watch. The night passes without incident, but I stayed up all night, for the second night in a row. I plan on staying up at night for the time being until I know that it is safe to sleep. They start putting me on medication. I meet with a social worker and my mother, he says to the two of us,

"We are putting Denis on medicine and he seems to be responding very well to it."

By the end of the week I fall into a routine; smoke a cigarette every few hours on smoke breaks, group meetings and meals; so, I'm confused when after putting me on different more potent medication a nurse walks into my room and says,

"They are ready for you know *now* Denis."

I follow her into the next room the nurse leaves. I take a seat among my fellow patients and notice that there is no one working for the hospital in the group meeting.

I don't know what I was thinking, but I decide to intentionally not listen to what anyone says in the group meeting. They all talk with a businesslike demeanor while I intentionally block them out.

They ask me something and I just say,

"No."

The man says something else directly to me and then I say, "No." again.

I start to pay attention to what they are saying. A woman with dark black hair and a petite build says,

"What are you going to do about your father? What are you going to do about your doctor? What are you going to do about your brother? What are you going to do about Trey?"

Someone interrupts her and tells her to stop talking.

I say, "I don't know, without them how am I going to pay for school. Are you going to?"

The man in charge of the meeting says, "No," then addresses the rest of the group.

He says, "Without Denis some of you might want to leave. You can leave as long as you sign these contracts."

A couple of people shuffle off to the side and sign some sort of contract. I leave the room and the rest of the patients that weren't in the group meeting are lined up to take medication. A couple of patients from New York grimace at me as I leave the meeting as they cut in line to get their pills. I make a beeline to the bathroom and puke my brains out.

The voices say, "I get it now, you tripping. What's next?"

I leave the hospital. My life continues, I talk to Tiff over email and call her every once in a while. I still love her. I think about returning to school at some point. I visit my school to try to get back in. I guess I didn't interview well with the Assistant Dean so they don't let me return to school. I try to make plans to get coffee with Tiff, but she cannot meet up until after my flight leaves. I reschedule my flight to meet up with her. She picks me up from a friend's house. As always, I'm astounded by the way she looks. She's dressed in a tan, skin colored collared shirt and hot pants. Even in casual clothing, she takes my breath away. She has long black hair, blue eyes and long legs. This is the first time we've met in person since I left school and I can tell that she's not happy to see me. I get into her blue beamer and she takes off, going zero to sixty in no time and swerves into the other lane. Driving at a ridiculous speed in a residential area

I remain calm, she looks to me, furious, but at the same time somewhat confused, she asks,

"You know that we're driving on the wrong side of the road, don't you?"

I say placidly, "Yes I do."

She says under her breath, "suicide," slows down and drives more smoothly.

At the coffee shop I can't get much out of her, she doesn't want to see me I can tell and she doesn't want to talk to me. I finally ask,

"Are you hungry? Let's go to Subway."

She says, "Alright"

In the sub shop she looks at me and says,

"Denis, these are our lives and we deserve to be with one another."

I should have said something different, I should have agreed with her and trusted her the way I have never really trusted another person. But instead I said,

"I'm sorry."

That seemed to set Tiff off, she started cursing at me

and making a scene at the restaurant,

"You fucking loser, you're throwing your life away. You

don't care about anyone but yourself. Why would anyone

ever want to go out with you, you disgust me." She goes on

this tangent for about five to ten minutes and I look at her,

feeling crushed and worthless, but I was determined not to

show it on my face. After her tongue lashing she asks,

"What, what do you have to say."

I answer, "I love you," with a smile.

She gives me a look, wondering where I got off, or if I was

just that stupid and says,

"Why? Why would you say that to me right now?"

I say with a grin,

"I don't know, you just seemed so beautiful to me just then."

She starts to cry. And I take her by the arm and exit

the restaurant and head towards the car. As she's crying she

asks me, "These are our lives. Why can't we be together?"

I answer immediately with a thought that had been swirling

around my head for a while. I had been so hurt by this whole

situation, I considered myself damaged goods so I say to Tiff,

"It's better for you this way, forget about me." And she

looks into my eyes piercing my soul and says back,

"Why, is it better for me this way?"

I don't know what to say

She asks, "Do you know what that means."

I look up into the sky as if reflecting on God and my

existence and answer her,

"Yes, I do."

I think it means that my life would change for the

worse. I think it means that I will not be able to get what I

want out of life from here on out. But knowing what it

meant and experiencing this are two far different things. So, I

take her by the arm and lead her to the car. She turns to me

to say something and I kiss her, passionately. I don't know if

this made her feel better or worse, but I ask,

"Are you alright to drive?"

Tiff says that I better drive. We return back to the house I'm staying at. I leave a few hours later.

The voices say, "Sometimes your best just ain't good enough. Shall we proceed?"

A few months pass and I'm starting to get my life back together. I see a psychiatrist. I try to get over Tiff. I seem to be making progress until the night I suddenly lose my mind. I wake up for a split second with Tiff is riding on top of me, stark naked, giving me an intense look. She looks away and my eyes shut again and I lose consciousness. I feel the most intense feeling I've ever had in my entire life while unconscious. I wake up and hear people talking in hushed tones in my hallway, I try to get up but can't move. I summon all of the power I possess and stumble into the bathroom. I hear footsteps rush to my brother's room as I stagger into the bathroom and try to clean myself off, but before I can use the wash cloth I start to lose consciousness. I stumble back into my bed and pass out.

I awake the next day and go to work wondering if I had some sort of wet dream, but if it was a dream, why did it feel so real? A few days later I wake up for a split second with someone holding my nose shut and placing a crack pipe in my mouth making me inhale, then black out again. I'm completely out of it. And then you started to talk to me.

Ch.4 Crazy Not Crazy

The voices say, "So you were crazy for not being crazy. I guess that would make sense if you weren't some motherfuckering asshole."

I go ballistic. This is the sixth night that I haven't slept. I have to go to work tomorrow. In my anger I get the voices to stop talking. I start imagining things that don't make sense, like underground submarines and people that live in the walls. The voices say in an astonished tone, "He did it to himself." I assume that they are talking about me being booted.

I start to see things in my head that I can tell aren't real but really freak me out. I see to children of the corn looking kids inside my closet, even though my closet is closed. I slam my palm into the door to try to rid of this hallucination. My parents wake up and we get into a shouting match.

Let me explain the theory I have about my life: we are all born with things we have to live with even if it isn't physical; in these matters no one is immune. If this is possible then it's true. My parents are calling his psychiatrist on the phone before I go to work. I had become paranoid and haven't been able to sleep. My parents yell at me about missing my psychiatrist appointment yesterday. I raise my voice and yell back at them. My father goes into the car to have a cigarette and I go ballistic. When he returns from the car I explain to him,

"You can't do this to me, you can't sabotage my fucking life like this, now move your fucking car."

He and I lock glares he presses his head against mine. I grill him and push his head against the wall with my head.

I can't leave because they are blocking my car in. My parents call the police. I talk to the officer for about a minute before I tell the officer that he can't arrest me when I'm in my house and try to walk away. The officer grabs my arm and before I can react the officer wrestles me to the ground. He puts my wrists in handcuffs, but the handcuffs are too tight and on backwards. They lead me to the cruiser backwards also. My parents are telling the officers that I attacked my father. The officer reads me my rights. An ambulance arrives at the scene. The officer says, "You can go to the mental institution or be charged for assaulting an officer and resisting arrest."

I reply, "I want to go to the mental institution."

The officer fixes the handcuffs so my hands aren't in them backwards, leads me into the ambulance and then handcuffs me to a gurney. The officer accompanies me to the hospital. I calm down in the ambulance and it is a quiet ride. I only speak to ask the officer to loosen the handcuffs, as I'm losing circulation in my shackled hand.

At the emergency room a doctor talks to me. The doctor takes my blood. I start to go into delirium or psychosis. This is the fourth time in a month that doctors have taken my blood. I hadn't slept in a week and had barely eaten anything in days.

I go off on the voices. I give them what for. With an exterior that is silent, but barely held together, I scream internally at the voices in my head. I read them the riot act, I give them a piece of my mind; I give them no quarter. I sit in a room in a hospital gown on a gurney for a long time. A security guard sits outside my room reading a book. After 7 hours in the emergency room they take me to the psych ward. I remember signing something for them to admit me.

That night I'm is not sure what is real and what isn't. I feverishly lie in bed surrounded by a curtain in a ward with twenty other men. I keep hearing gunshots in the distance.

Suddenly the curtains part and I see a vampire. I don't believe in vampires but that is what I see; a tall man in black garments with a baldhead and fangs. He approaches me, and I don't move. He puts his face up against mine and asks,

"Can I kiss you?"

I just nod, wondering when and how this was all going to end. He kisses me then leaves. A little later Tiff enters the curtained area and lies in bed with me. I wanted to kiss her but I was barely awake, so I just held her for a long time. I pass out and when I come to she's gone. Moments later a man I don't recognize enters into the curtained area. He has a knife. I know that if I move he'll just stab me so I remain still, clinging to life in more ways than one. The armed man gets on top of me, puts his knees on my hands and places the knife to my throat. I just glare at my would-be murderer and think to myself that if he cuts my throat I'm going to bite his throat. It isn't realistic, but I hate this man with every ounce of my being for wanting to kill me. It seems that I feel the knife against my throat for twenty minutes, I imagine myself as a wolf biting this random person, who is about to kill me. Then as suddenly as he entered the curtained area he leaves.

My thinking becomes more and more faint until it is gone. I am dead. There is no bright light or anything it's more like a feeling that I had never experienced before. I have a feeling that reminds me of peace. I have an out of body experience. I hear two men talking to me, one says,

"Wake up, just blink your eyes if you are there. If you don't we are going to have to use defibulators to resuscitate you. It could kill you if you're not dead already."

I try to open my eyes but I'm dead. I hear the two men leaving and saying to one another,

"This kid's life sucks anyways, let's just leave him."

This galvanizes me to come back alive.

I walk out of the room and look at the nurse expecting him to say something to me, but he doesn't. No one mentions the fact that EMT's left me for dead. I ask another nurse for some Aspirin. I heard once before that

Aspirin thins the blood; I hope that it might help the cause. I can barely feel my left leg. I spend the rest of the day running back and forth in the room with the beds and hope that the increased circulation it will keep me alive. Finally, one of the attendants approaches me and asks if I want to play a card game. He teaches me how to play spades. I spend a lot of the rest of my time there playing spades with the staff in the psych ward and recovering from that horrible night.

Occasionally I have a meeting with my parents, doctors and social workers. They say that I need to sign a form to request to leave. I think that this is bullshit and vaguely remember signing myself into the mental institution. I believe that they will have to let me leave in two weeks if I don't sign anything else. So, I say that I don't want to request to leave, as I might want to stay longer. After two weeks they let me go.

I leave the in-patient program and enter an outpatient program near my house. I have meetings with my psychiatrist and parents where we frequently argue about me going to another hospital for a diagnosis. I don't have much fight left in me so I cave and agree to go to another hospital that my parents' friend runs to see the "magnificent seven," a team of elite doctors, who give me the diagnosis of schizophrenia.

The voices are getting more belligerent.

One voice tells me, "You're designated to die."

Another voice says, "You could be better off. You could live. There's a better place than where you're at now."

Intuitively I believe the second voice. The voices are more internal after the night in the hospital. However, one night I see in my mind's eye the Grim Reaper with its hood on. It gets more and more real. I see Death and he takes off his hood. It's just a skull with a snake running through the eye sockets with its sickle off to the side. Abstractly this isn't scary, but in actuality it nearly frightens me to death. I grill the Grim Reaper anyways. Later that night I see what seems like an alternate reality where a projection of myself and of the voices exist. A group of people huddle around me.

I start falling down into an abyss. As I fall I see groups of people at different levels of my fall huddling around my precipitous drop just jeering at me.

About a week later I go to bed for the night. I am still recovering from not sleeping for a week and whatever happened to me that night in the hospital. I am exhausted and hoping for a good night's rest. I awaken suddenly. The door to my closet is slowly opening. I just go back to sleep, thinking that my mind is playing tricks on me. Another creek from my closet door wakes me again. This time I get up to see what's opening the door. There, standing in front of me in the closet is a man, who's about 6 4"in a Jason mask holding a butcher knife. Before I freak out and get myself killed, in a serene moment, I decide to meditate. For ten minutes, myself and what I assume is a serial killer just grill each other, while I enter a trance. For a split second the masked man in the closet disappears. The man reappears and I consider reaching out and trying to feel if he is real with my hands, but I do not. I think that he looks as about as real as real could be in that moment. The first thing that comes to mind in this meditative state is that I'm hungry. So, I tell the killer in the closet,

"I better go and make myself a peanut butter and jelly sandwich."

He replies in a gruff voice, "Why don't you do that."

Turning his back to him I exit my bedroom, walk down the stairs and into my kitchen. I get the peanut butter and jelly out of the fridge and begin making a sandwich. I hear the person coming down the stairs. When I turn around, the man is stalking down the hallway. He's taking long strides and swaying back and forth, almost in a berserker like fashion and brandishing a huge knife. As he tries to stab me with all his force, in one motion I block his thrust with my right hand and punch the man in the throat with my left. The man in the Jason mask goes down like a sack of potatoes and lies on the kitchen floor unconscious.

I don't unmask the man, because I don't want to find out if this is real. Whether it is real or not, it doesn't seem to matter. I think of calling the police but don't. Getting arrested by the police is still fresh in my mind, so I take away his knife, realizing that it's from my kitchen and begin to walk back upstairs. I look into the den and sees my father, just sitting there watching TV. I shake my head in dismay and walk up the stairs and go back to sleep in my brother's vacant room. My dad can't hear very well; I think to myself that might be the issue. Not sure whether the man who accosted me in my home is dead or alive I go to sleep, with the knife under my pillow, and wake up the next day as if nothing happened.

After another day at the out-patient program, I walk to a store near my house. Two people, a man and a woman, emerge from the woods nearby. They wear rags and appear drunk. That's not what catches my eye. What catches my eye is that the woman's jaw was black, like from gangrene and locked open. It is like her jaw is rotting off of her face. I don't really care. I'm numb to life. I walk behind them as they walk to the liquor store. I go to the pharmacy and buy a pack of smokes. As I walk back to my house, I walk past the two of them sitting on a bench and I try to muster the curiosity to look at the grotesque woman but I cannot.

One night I take a walk around my neighborhood. It is a cool summer night. As I walk down a hill I remember the time I had crashed my bike on this same street when I was a kid. I was maybe nine years old and peddling like crazy down the hill, reaching max speed. Suddenly, a car pulls into a driveway directly in front of me. I try to stop but I'm going too fast and I get flipped over the hood of this man's car. The man in the car was kind enough to walk me and my bike back to my house. In the middle of reminiscing about my childhood I turn around and see something out of the corner of my eye. It is the vampire from the night in the hospital. Like something you would see out of a horror movie, this vampire is rapidly crawling towards me. The crawl is so unnatural, not like any animal's or human's movements should be. It looks like the devil is moving him.

As he grabs my ankle, I look down at his face and say, "Gollum?"

I was just trying not to lose my shit and that is what came to mind at that time. Gollum is a character from "Lord of the Rings."

The vampire looks up at me and says, "Yes, Gollum."

Then I stomp his face with my boots and keep on walking. I guess that this stops the vampire from stalking me since I am able to return back home without any further incident.

The voices are talking to me from when I wake up to when I go to sleep now, and I'm having crazy nightmares too. The medication doesn't stop the onslaught of chatter or my eye from blinking rapidly. If I am unable to continue talking somehow then it feels like the voices will take control, I worry. I talk, argue and scrap. I try to understand why the voices are so murderously angry. I come up with a theory, that I'm trapped in almost a cage fight to the death with voices. I call this theory Time-is-mass. Time is mass basically means that the voices and my consciousness are a part of a group. There is a finite amount of time for a voice or me to talk and only one of us can talk at a time. So, I start to try and filibuster.

These are the perils one risks in order to live life. Perhaps, if I were to enter back into the rat race, I would succeed. Though the terrible consequences of failure make me have second thoughts. As I try to find my voice once again, thought to be forever lost at times, through others, and myself I gather strength.

Love is transcendent. It can lift you out of any situation with newfound direction and purpose. As much as I've tried to reject it, love is real. It cannot be denied. I always believed that when I found love it would fix all my problems. But love doesn't do that. Love makes you do crazy things. I think that I don't want to be bitter about my life.

People, who make choices, often do so out of fear. Though being smart doesn't mean that you know the future, being wary of certain outcomes makes sense. Equally, the passing of time depicts your life. I think about why I am the way I am. Whether through conditioning or evolution we are made to react to our impulses and are defined by human nature. It's like we're programmed or hardwired to be ourselves. An example of this is that a lot of us would be awestruck in seeing magnificent pieces of art, like the "David" by Michelangelo and cannot react in any other way.

In everyday life we are guided by impulses, which affect our thoughts and actions. If one were to have a bird's eye view of this "hardwiring" they would see that in order to live life one must function by using these directives to their benefit. As much as we want to take the high road, be peaceful, rise up from our condition, we cannot cast out the human condition. Though there's no methodology for determining how someone will react every time, one can make a pretty good guess in some circumstances. A person touches an electric outlet and gets a shock; it's likely that they won't touch it again.

I hope that one day I will be able to think back to when I was really sick and read this journal in order to get a glimpse of what I was like. I try to understand the rules that govern what I am going through in my head. As my mind deteriorates I go deep into its recesses. I go into something I call Metaphysicality. This is an imaginary world where I fight my enemies. It is where I battle in my mind to remain sane. In there, reality is defined by four laws, which I invented. I call the four laws the Powerulic Government. Those four rules are as follows: 1.) Everybody gets to make rules. 2.) You don't have to listen or follow rules. 3.) Rules have to define inexplicable power 4.) There are no rules after this rule. I'm not sure the overall meaning of the powerulic government; it simply describes what my mind is going through at this time.

I write some more in my journal:

Life is struggling. Living desperation, I extend who I am. My life is hard. Self-doubt seeps through my confidence. My mind goes from one place to another and I wonder how I got to the place that I am. I like to ponder over who I am and lately I can't. Inconspicuous thoughts creep into my mind and I lose them before I can grab them. So, I think and talk about ideas that are blatant and hope that people understand what I infer about. I need to get back to normal. Ideas disjointedly cloud my cognitive ability. It scares me to make progress because I need to have it in the right direction. I'm afraid when I think about a bunch of ideas that I can't really support. But I think I'm on the right track.

I cannot find the truth alone. My story is unique, but by connecting to other people, I become a part of something larger. Knowing the truth would explain a lot about why I'm the way I am. Knowing what really happened to me, or if I'm just delusional, explains the decisions I've made with my life. If I find the truth, then maybe I can avoid keep making the same mistakes over and over again. I want an explanation as to why these things might have happened to me; maybe if

I understand, I can prevent them from happening to me or to other people.

It's a one and a million shot that I'll get what I want out of life. The odds are stacked up against me. I've fought the odds and won before. But I've also lost. Nothing can erase what I've been through. What drives me at my weakest moments is the thought there's still justice, honor and loyalty in the world. I'm loyal in my heart to those who have or still do love me. I want to live life to its fullest. It's just this doubt hackles me to where I am right now. If I don't reach my place, I might die trying, that's how hard I've fought for things in life.

Under pressure from my psychiatrist, I go to what was described to me as a three-quarters-of-a-way house; basically, it is a half-way house for rich people. Even though I have reservations, the staff has me sign a contract stating that I will stay there for two years. It is a dual-diagnosis facility, where they talk about mental health, drug and alcohol addiction. I get acclimated to my new environment.

It is okay, but every night right before curfew, while I'm having my last cigarette one of the other patients screams into the night on the back porch. It seems to me that he's yelling at the voices in his head, but I'm not sure. He screams,

"Get out! Get the fuck out of my house!"

Nobody else pays much attention, but I continue having my nightly cigarette before curfew, watching this 6"3 man screaming while moving his arms in a throwing gesture every night as if physically throwing someone out of the house.

I decide that this isn't the kind of help I need at this point. I talk to the social worker a lot and convince him to have a meeting with my parents in two weeks to consider all of my options. I know that I will have to have a really good almost flawless argument, and that I would have to refute all the counter-arguments and concerns my parents would have. I wonder how I will be able to do this with the voices disrupting my train of thought constantly. I come up with a dialectic similar to Marx's. I think of all the counter arguments and worries my parents might have. I come up with an anti-thesis for these counter-arguments, then an anti-conclusion and all the supporting arguments in between. I start compiling pages of these refutations to all the arguments I think my parents will deploy using this dialectic I partially borrow from Marx. One night before the meeting with my parents, I have a sex dream about Tiff.

I wake up the next day feeling strange. I go to the bathroom next to my room. I have never had anal sex before but on the toilet, it seems to me that I am experiencing its after-affects. Knowing that my best option is to just leave and not deal with this I prepare my argument as best I can all things considered. The meeting with my parents is a success, I'm allowed to return home with certain conditions including that I will quit smoking pot.

Ch. 5 Windmills

Some of the voices in my head assume the identity of people from my school. One of these classmates' voices takes it upon himself to occupy my face. This involves individual voice's moving different sections of my face. For example, one voice makes my right eye blink, another the left, another my cheeks and so on. The classmate from school occupies the center of my forehead. This lasted maybe a week. This particular classmate voice gives me a lot of trouble. He puts me through what he calls "Saw". "Saw" involves me talking to serial killer voices. Not only does he put me through "Saw" one but through all the sequels throughout my time dealing with him. Nonetheless, the classmate voice that gives me the most trouble is Trey. Trey talks endlessly about Treytopia, where only people named Trey can be in charge.

Trey voice is talking about Treytopia one day, when he decides to put me through some shit. I am in my living room and Trey says,

"This is the power of Treytopia! I'm going to Ka-Chink you!"

Then I blink and hear a sound like ice cracking in my head. I open my eyes and hear the ice cracking again. Trey says,

"In Treytopia, if you close your eyes and I Ka-Chink you, you can't open your eye's permanently. If you have your eyes open and I Ka-Chink you, you cannot close your eyes ever again. If you pass I'll give you a grade."

So, for maybe forty-five minutes I open and close my eyes; trying to blink when the Trey voice wants my eyes open and opening my eyes when he desires them shut. Every time he tries to permanently open or close my eyes I can hear the sound of ice cracking. I don't want to find out if Trey voice can make good on his threats so I persist. It's nerve-wracking to say the least. After putting me through that hell Trey voice begrudgingly gives me a B- and stops.

Around a year after I start to hear the voices something happens in my mind, or in Metaphysicality. I become Godded into life, I am no longer designated to die. The voices all but stop for one summer and I am able to get good marks in two classes at a local community college. The Godded into life voices turn sour at my cousins wedding in Florida though. I accidently pack a mismatch of dress shoes for the trip. I am such a mess I miss the ceremony buying new dress shoes with my parents. As a result of this fiasco, I am no longer Godded into life, according to the voices, but I don't know if I am designated to die still or not.

I start creating strategies to combat the voices, it turns into a huge war of attrition. In my auditory hallucination world "Star Wars" is the name of the game. There are two groups of bigtime voices, the rebels and the empire. I used to be a rebel because of my father, but the voices tell me that I am now a part of the empire now. I wasn't having any of that so I start a revolution among the indigenous aliens and clean house.

At around this time I bring evenness to the force. I'm not really sure how I do it, but the voices are really impressed. They are so impressed that one of the voices initiates a sexual, Metaphysical encounter. I feel like I am an animal and that the voice is melding its animal essence in with mine. It was overall an incredible feeling.

I play a game with the voices. All the voices count me out, but I play for keeps. My skills against the voices has steadily risen. I start having terrible nightmares while I'm in the game. I have this one nightmare that really sticks with me.

I see a body of water and a shack near the edge. I approach the shack thinking,

"How am I going to get across the water?"

I see a crow siting on a chair outside the shack. It starts talking to me. Abstractly, this isn't a big deal, but the voice of the crow sends chills down my spine. The crow explains,

"You want to go across the water but your friends are holding you back. You should go across the water and fulfill your destiny."

I wake up screaming at the cackling sound from the crow's voice.

The next day, I make my way through the "dungeon" in Metaphysicality, projecting my image and the voices images into an alternate reality, where I have some control. I reach the end. I don't want to go to the final part it feels wrong. So, I see a line that I don't cross and I sit down and read a book I imagine I hold. I see a spear and grab the spear, then stab the voice who was holding the spear. I win the game.

About a year and a half from my last hospitalization, my strategies for combating the voices reach surgical precision. At this stage, some voices some willing to help me. So, I tell them what to do. I tell the voices helping me to say a phrase or two that sounds like something their voice group would say. Then the next voice says something that is similar, but goes a little deeper into the meaning of what the first voice said. Given a little time and a little momentum, the voices helping me would thunder scathing remarks that shook the other voices to their core. I call this the personality strategy. I plan on making the dominoes fall. To start off I threaten the bigtime voices, voices whose identity I'm unsure of but have clout. I say to them,

"I'm going to hit you, unless you threaten someone else with the same threat I'm making to you."

I hear the bigtime voices threaten the next voice group.

The bigtime voices say, "I'm going to hit you, unless you threaten someone else with the same threat I'm making to you."

It goes all the way down the pecking order. Then I start a chain-reaction. I execute my threat by hitting the big-time voices with my personality strategy leaving them little choice except to execute their threat; all the way down the line voices hit each other. It made me happy, but the voices are irate after the dust settles. It sounds like to me that they are not fucking around anymore and they planned to close ranks on me. I know I'm in deep shit so I try for the second time to get back to normal.

I had tried maybe a month or two in to fix my head. I knew it wouldn't work, but I had to try. Every other time I even thought of trying to "get back to normal" the voices would go haywire, making me blink and break my concentration. This time it's different, the voices are distracted from my domino tactic. First, I try to move my mind away from the voices. This fails. Then I have an idea. I do the opposite of moving away from the voices and move into them. This also fails to make a difference. Then it occurs to me that I should try moving away and into the voices at the same time. This seems to make a difference. I keep on doing this, fighting with the voices and moving into and away from them at the same time, every waking hour for a week.

At the end of the week I'm making real headway, I am also in a cab in New York City visiting my brother, who just moved there. In this cab I have a spiritual experience. I gravitate towards an orb; I look around and see other orbs, I can't really think but I try to make the orb come to my reality. It works, the voices are upset. They start talking differently from normal. One voice says something and another completes the sentence. They are all talking at the same time and not understanding what's going on. The voices lost most of their power over me.

I'm in a state of limbo for about six months, where I slowly regain some of my cognitive abilities. It's 2007 now, I'd been hearing voices in my head for about two years. I think that I will get back to "normal" relatively soon. However, in the meantime I want to do what the voices were doing to me to them, and I don't really care how it works out in the end. For the past six months I had been saying to the voices that what they believed in was bullshit. They couldn't talk over me or combat me for talking time anymore. I think that I understand how the voices operate. They were simply turning the way I functioned into something else, into bullshit. So, I thought I could do the same to them in kind. Over the past six months I had been thinking of all the different ways I functioned, like the way I eat, or the way I dream, or the way I smile, etc. and trying to apply it to the way the voices functioned. For example, I would say in my head the way I breathe is the way I tell time and vice versa. I know that this doesn't make any sense, but I wasn't making sense on purpose, just to piss off the voices. It didn't matter, I was getting back to normal soon anyways.

Now I'm at my Dad's office zoning out, talking to the voices sitting in a chair while my Dad works at his desk and another employee uses the copier. What is happening in the office barely registers. I am explaining to a voice inside my head about how I was racially insensitive at one point as a teenager. I explain that I thought that since I had a few black friends that this meant that I was down with black people as a whole. I am in the process of explaining why this is wrong. I get a feeling that I am going to get back to normal in the next moment or two, but I want to finish my thought. So, as I'm finishing explaining to the voices the how it took a lot of soul searching to realize the error of my ways, I stop talking inside my head and wait for the triumph of being able to think clearly and not having to blink, or "hear" voices anymore, the employee who's making copies abruptly finishes her work. She turns around and the exact second that was supposed to be my triumph, and has some sort of interaction with me, I'm not sure what. The end result is a rush of energy inside my head, but it is blocked by something going on in real life. I feel shock, horror and dread. I franticly try to think of ways to rectify what just happened, but come up empty. It feels like an integral part of me, the part that was able to fight the voices, my own voice has been ripped from me. I see what looks like a string of pearls, that reminds me of my spine float up into the ether. All the emotion, what is at this moment pain suddenly felt hollow as something hard to explain happened to my throat. What feels like my emotional self leaves by way of my throat and chest. I think to myself, there's no way I can bounce back from this. I go into a state of disbelief and I am completely shell-shocked. A few days later the financial crisis of 07'-08' begins.

What else can I do but soldier on. I move out of my parent's house and live with two old friends from high school, Sanjiv and Emily who are in a relationship, in Boston proper. I continue working for my parents' business. I still have a lot of issues, but I'm much less irritable and can relate a little better to people, as opposed to when I was a war inside my head. I am somewhat traumatized from my experience, at times I can still feel the knife against my throat from the hospital, I think of the missed connection with Tiff, and I dwell on the position I am in. But, I continue working for my parents' business and think about returning to school. The voices stop making sense. It seemed as though they lost interest in me after my defeat. The only thing that they would say to me now is "Yeah, that's exactly it." Over and over again. A part of me is still there, I can feel myself out in the ether of my mind, but I've changed. I make a promise to myself to pick up the pieces, but I can tell that what is driving me is revenge, not towards the random employee who distracted me at such a pivotal moment, but towards the voices.

I enter into community college, but it's still difficult for me to read and write papers. I feel like I have changed so much since I had been at the college in Florida and that I need to relearn how to do school again. I can't function as well as I used to, but I am a lot humbler and more self-aware. I read a book about some climbers who survived a huge storm on Mt. Everest. A climber with a broken leg managed to climb down the mountain during a snow storm back to base camp. He said in the book that he would pick points a small distance away and make it his goal to reach that point.

He did this exercise all the way back to base camp. I think to myself that if I choose small goals one at a time, like making to class on time, starting homework earlier than the night before its due, and not skipping any classes, I can achieve more than if I focused on larger goals. My dad articulates my situation succinctly in one family therapy meeting.

He says, "Denis has to make more with less."

I say to myself that my mental health is my highest priority. But I make little progress on that front. I focus my attention on school, while my mental health remains on the back burner. Thwarted in the mental health aspect of my life, I start thinking of life in terms of functioning. I can't function very well, and I think this is the reason I wasn't doing well in my classes. I forget assignments and not write them down, and am disorganized. I continue working for my parents' business and pass maybe half my courses and dropping the other half before the add/drop deadline. The next semester I take a class in organization. It seems remedial, but I think it is worth a try.

In the organization class there is someone who seems like they are going through the same issues that I went through just a short time ago. He moves erratically and blinks constantly, but it seems like he is really trying in class. He has an aide, who goes with him to class to write down notes and help him out in general. I'm not sure what his diagnosis is but he gives me some inspiration.

I think to myself, "If this person, who is right in the thick of having serious issues can pass this class and take it seriously, so can I."

In class the professor tasks us to memorize all the presidents of the United States. One day, the professor calls on us individually, asking each student to recall five presidents in order. We get to President Ulysses S. Grant then the professor calls on me to list the next five presidents.

I say, "Rutherford Hayes, James Garfield, Chester Arthur, Grover Cleveland, and…. And…"

I draw a blank and the professor says, "Think very carefully, the next thing you say could make or break your academic career."

I try to think. It's really hard for me to focus. I dig deep and remember the answer.

I say confidently "Benjamin Harrison."

The professor says, "Very good."

I say, "Did that answer make or break my career."

He says, "I'm not sure."

I had come up with an answer on the spot, which I was having trouble with. It gives me confidence that I can recall information under pressure, which is a big difference from my earlier classes at community college. With this ego boost I do better than I had the previous semester. Piece by piece I attempt to put back together my life.

A few months later, I have tickets to the Jay Z concert at TD Garden. I had bought the tickets way back, when I was still in limbo, expecting that this would be a celebration

Ch 6 KO'd

of sorts when I got back to "normal." I go to the concert with my roommates and one of their friends.

Ch. 6 KO'd

One night, my roommate Emily and I decide to get tattoos together. Our friend Adam comes along for the ride. I had been thinking of getting a tattoo for a while, something that would signify what I went through. I decide to get the letters "KO" in plain lettering and black ink tattooed on my chest. The "KO" stands for knocked out. I want the tattoo to be a reminder of what I went through. My heart is still broken over Tiffany and I'm not sure that I am even capable of loving someone like I did with her anymore. The tattoo signifies that will never forget the way I am now and what brought me here. I know that this is a monumental task, but I remind myself of how close I was to achieving the impossible. I think that I can eventually accomplish my goal of becoming conscious eventually, and without much help, which is the only way I've learned to deal with my issues.

As I sit in the chair and the tattoo artist gets to work, the saying, "It is better to have loved and lost then to have never loved at all" comes to mind. I'm not sure if this is the case for me, but it still rings true in my mind. By now I am pretty much sane and looking back at what I have been through is hard. I know there are things that I went through that couldn't be real, like the delusions about being a drug dealer, the vampire and the voices in my head. I can't really come to much of a conclusion as to what I went through, in terms of if it really happened or if it was all in my head. So, the tattoo also represents my current thinking about my ordeal, I can't understand it, understanding doesn't seem to get me anywhere, so I will continue to be "knocked out" or unable to understand what I went through.

I can't help ruminating over what I went through with the voices. I get into the habit of driving my car late at night aimlessly for hours on end all around Boston. I am driving in Mattapan one night and have to take a piss. It is an emergency. I stop by a parking lot on a side street and take a piss by a chain link fence. Suddenly, when I'm done, I see a police light flashing. Two Boston beat police officers exit their car. They search me and my car. I get back into my car while the two officers walk over towards an abandoned car. I hear a loud smash. The two officers approach my car and have me get out.

The first police officer says, "What are you doing in Mattapan at three O'clock in the morning? Are you trying to score some drugs?"

I say, "No, couldn't sleep. Sometimes when I can't sleep I take a drive."

The police officer says, "Bullshit, what were you doing by the fence over there?"

I say, "I had to take a piss and didn't know where to stop so I went over there."

The police officer says, "Do you know how dangerous Mattapan is at night? We have a police station right around the block and there's still murders that happen all the time around here. I don't believe you were just taking a drive."

I say, "Yeah I know how dangerous it is. I heard someone got stabbed a few years back right across the street from the police station."

The officer asks, "Do you have any significant mental issues that I should be aware of?"

I say, "Uh, yeah I do. I'm schizophrenic."

The officer says, "Show me where you took a piss."

I wonder to myself why they would be asking me where I took a piss. Instinctively I walk over to a nearby wall instead of the real location and say,

"I took a piss by this wall."

The officer says, "I don't see any piss. Your story isn't checking out."

I say, "I forgot, I took a piss over here."

I walk over to the chain link fence and show him. Then we walk back towards my car. By the abandoned car, in a direct line from where I took the piss to where I parked my car there is some broken glass that I avoid stepping on.

The second officer says, "Why did you smash the window?"

I say, "What are you talking about?"

The officer says, "Did you smash the car window with your fist or your feet. Lift up your shoes."

I comply and the officer asks, "Why is there glass on your shoe?"

I look at the shoe then at the officer and say, "I don't see any glass on my shoes."

Then I lift up my other shoe, which is also free of glass. The officers converse between themselves for a minute and then talk to me.

The second officer says, "We're going to have to write a report about how we found you by the abandoned car, where an incident of destruction of property occurred. You are going to have to leave your car here. You can come back and get it tomorrow."

I thank my lucky stars and call a cab back to my apartment. A few weeks later my old friend, Adam is going transferring to a college in Argentina, and some of our friends get together at a bar in Boston to see him off. A wave of anxiety hits me at the bar. I don't know what hits me, but I can't be there anymore. I get in my car and start driving, hoping this anxiety will go away. The voices I usually can ignore get louder and require more of my attention. I get on the highway. I feel like if I stop driving then I will break down. I drive through the night and through most of the next day. In Georgia, I see a muscle car speeding and I speed up with him. As the muscle car slows down and as I drive by I see a state police officer turn on his lights. He pulls me over and writes me up. I continue driving and end up in South Carolina, at which point I stop and check into a motel. I call my parents and tell them that I drove to Charleston and I am unsure why. We get ahold of my psychiatrist, who phones in a prescription to a pharmacy near my motel. My brother Andrew gets on a plane from New

York City to drive me and my car back to Boston. He arrives later that day and we go to the pharmacy to pick up my medication. The drive back is mostly silent.

Even though I believe the drive mostly had to do with unresolved issues from my ordeal with the voices, I make up a story to my doctor that I had drove down to South Carolina, because of a superstition I had about the Red Sox. On a bridge on the Jamaica Way, a busy street in Boston, for years there had been graffiti saying, "Reverse the Curse" over a reverse curve sign. The graffiti referred to the Curse of the Bambino. The Curse of the Bambino was supposed to be the reason that the Red Sox hadn't won the World Series for 86 years, because the team became cursed when they traded Babe Ruth to the Yankees. It was washed over after the Red Sox won the World Series in 2004, around the time of my first hospitalization. I tell Dr. Brown that I had driven all that way to "reverse the curse." He accepts this answer. I continue keeping a lot of my issues to myself.

My parents become more worried about me living on my own, where I start to develop a bad weed habit again. I am honest with my treatment team about it and they recommend that I move back into the family home so that I can kick marijuana. I move back home after about two years of living on my own and sincerely try to kick pot. I start seeing a specialist in addiction recovery, named Gary, in an out-patient program. I am diagnosed with marijuana dependency. I can go a week or maybe a month at a time without smoking pot, then my will power gives out and I smoke. The addiction recovery specialist is getting frustrated with me about my pot use after about six months. One day I tell Gary about how I got mugged.

I'm about twelve years old hanging out on Newbury street with my friend, Fred. Fred and I thought that it was a good idea to try and score some pot. Back in the nineties Boston was much more dangerous than it is now. We see a group of teenagers, maybe ten or fifteen of them, walking down Mass Ave. holding a boom box blaring rap music. We approach them and ask if they had any weed for sale.

One of the teenagers says, "Yeah we got some trees, but we can't sell it to you on the street, follow us and we'll sell you a dub."

We follow the group to an alley about ten blocks down Mass Ave. On the walk to the alley I get a bad vibe and think about running away, but they surround us as we walked. In the alley, one of the teenagers reaches into his pants as if he's grabbing a bag of pot. But, instead of dealing us some weed he cold-cocks me in the face then pushes me into a large garbage bin, cutting up my shirt. I only had about ten dollars in my jacket, which I forgot about as soon as the teenager started wailing on me. He hit me about ten times, then whispered to me,

"Go down, go down already."

I can't think. I started yelling,

"Take my jacket, I don't have any money."

I look over and see as the rest of the group surround Freddy. He lies on the ground with one of the teenagers on top of him searching his clothes. Freddy has a tin full of cash but he had hidden it. Then the teenager punching me started hitting me again. Finally, we hear police sirens, the group of teenagers run in one direction down the alley and Freddy and I run in another. We walk back to Newbury Street.

Freddy says, "I had two hundred in my tin, but they only got twenty off of me. That wasn't that bad, was it?"

With my ears still ringing from the beating I play it tough and say, "No, it wasn't that bad."

As I finish the story, Gary gives me a snide look and says, "How long have you been waiting to tell me that story. I bet you tell that story to as many people that as you can."

I'm not sure what he means. I think about what he said and say,

"I'm schizophrenic, I've been through a lot of shit. I told you that story because I thought it was relevant to our conversation."

Gary says, "Being schizophrenic is no excuse to smoke pot."

I say, "I think that you're being biased against schizophrenic people. You know I have to deal with the stigma every day."

Gary is taken aback and tries to defend himself.

He says, "I'm not being biased I'm just saying that you can't use your mental illness as a crutch."

I say, "I think that you're being insensitive to my illness."

Eventually he apologizes to me, but it really upsets me. After this meeting, I uncover newfound resolve to quit smoking herb. It's incredibly hard the first few weeks, dealing with the boredom, and changing my social routine. I strategize, what time's I hang out with different friends and in what context. I only hang out with certain friends during the daytime and avoid plans for the most part at night, when I'm most tempted to smoke. When I get the pot out of my system for about a month I feel the benefits of my efforts. I can think a little more clearly and have a lot more energy.

The second month is pretty easy not smoking. It is the spring and I work for my parents' business most of the day. I feel like I've accomplished something, while quitting. I tell my friends that I quit herb. A few of them ask,

"Are you going to quit forever?"

I usually say, "No, but I want to quit for the foreseeable future."

After about three months I forget about all the reasons that I quit and the benefits seem to be minimal, even though it helps a lot being sober. I start smoking again. I tell my treatment team and they recommend rehab, so I admit myself into a rehab facility. I'm on summer break, I am not taking classes at community college this summer so I think that I can afford the time to spend a few weeks in rehab.

Ch. 7 The Definition

My first day of rehab I tell the group that I'm there for pot. I hear a loud scoff. I tell them that I can't smoke pot because I'm schizophrenic. The doctor heading the group tries to help me out by explaining that a lot of people whole *who* deal with drug and alcohol addiction are dual-diagnosed with a mental illness along with substance abuse addiction. This seems like bad news for the rest of the group, but they listen to the doctor's spiel. There are people there for opioid, coke and alcohol addiction mostly, I'm the only one there for weed. I go to the rehab outpatient program during the day and go to AA meetings at night. I try out a Narcotics Anonymous meeting, but I refuse to say I'm an addict. I don't think that I am an addict and listening to all of these horror stories about addiction to hard drugs makes me think that me being in rehab for pot is an insult to "real" drug abusers trying to sober up. But I try to maintain a humble attitude.

Every day, a different patient in rehab tells their history of drug abuse. It is my turn today and I have nothing prepared. I ask if I can postpone my sharing with the group

but the doctors say no. So, I sit in front of the group and tell

my history with drugs.

"So, the first time I drank alcohol I was ten years old.

My friend Fred and I had raided my parents liquor cabinet.

We thought we were being cool by drinking and getting

fucked up. I smoked my first joint when I was twelve. My

brother, Andrew, introduced me to pot with one of his friends.

We smoked in Cleveland Circle and hung out for a while.

By the age of thirteen I would get booze by paying homeless

people in Boston a tip for procuring me alcohol. I got drunk

a lot of weekends. I smoked pot every once in a while.

When I was sixteen I tried mushrooms for the first time and

had a bad trip. I had to go to school the next day. I tried

Coke for the first time when I was seventeen, which was

around the same time I started to smoke butts. My junior and

senior year of high school I pretty much smoked pot every

day, and did mushrooms two or three more times. Then the

summer before I went off to college I quit smoking herb and

cigs. But, I had trouble making friends my freshman year so after about eleven months I started smoking again. The next semester I joined a frat. There was a lot of binge drinking. I started to have mental issues the beginning of my sophomore year so I dropped out of school and came back home to Boston. I was diagnosed with Schizophrenia and I've been trying to reign in my pot use ever since, but it has been difficult. That's it, that's my history with drug use. Thanks for listening."

After I share with the group it's time for the other patients to react to my history. On a sheet of paper is a list of things that trigger drug abuse. Last on that list was the word, "insanity," followed by a definition: "Insanity is the mistake of doing the same thing over and over again and expecting different results." The doctors ask the group to pick a trigger from the list of ten that most relates to my history, as they ask after every sharing. As I sat in front of the group, person after person, about twenty people in all said, "insanity" was the reason that I used drugs. This didn't feel great but I put up with it because I didn't want to let anyone know how it hurt to have everyone in the room except for maybe the doctors to think that I was bat-shit crazy.

While I was in rehab, I hear the news that my maternal grandfather, Grandaddy died. He was old at the time of his death, ninety-eight years old, but it hit me pretty hard. I had fond memories of visiting him in Tampa as a child. After a couple of weeks in rehab, I finish the drug treatment program and fly down to Florida to attend his memorial. Grandaddy was a character. He was an accomplished amateur golfer at one time, who considered going pro, but his golf dreams were interrupted by the Great Depression. As a kid I remember Grandaddy would regale us with stories. When he was a teenager in the 1920's Grandaddy caddied for Babe Ruth in a tournament. Grandaddy said that Babe Ruth was winning the tournament, but at the turn he got drunk at the clubhouse and lost his lead on the back nine.

The memorial is held at the country club that Grandaddy belonged to, and where I had spent a lot of time at when I visited my mom's side of the family as a kid. One man approaches me and introduces himself.

He says, "Hi, you must be Irving's grandson, I'm Wyatt."

I shake his hand and say, "Hello Wyatt, nice to meet you."

Wyatt isn't satisfied with my handshake.

He says, "That's not how you shake a hand. Let's try this again."

I shake his hand again, this time a little harder, but Wyatt's grip crushes my hand.

Wyatt is still not satisfied with my handshake. He wants me to practice with him. After about seven handshakes we part ways. My dad comes up with the idea to give Grandaddy a twenty-one-golf drive salute at the country club to see him off properly. In the past this would have irritated me a lot. I think about the way I would have reacted to this touching tribute a few years ago, at age eighteen. I would have thought that my dad was imposing his own way of coping with Granddaddies' death on everyone else, that my dad was being selfish. At the point I am at now, I understand that this isn't just for show and that my dad had thought this through. I hear one of the mourners talking as we walk to the tee box.

He says, "I don't want to do this Jim. I don't like this."

Jim says, "Why not? It's sort of apropos for Irving's memorial."

The man says, "I don't know. I just don't feel comfortable."

At the tee box, twenty-one of us wait to make our drives, three at a time. When it is my turn I hit the ball about as far as I could hit it down the fairway.

When I leave the tee box, my Aunt says to me, "Your drive was probably the longest out of all of them."

I say, "Thanks, but I don't think that that is true."

I fly back to Boston and try to resume my life. I'm still in community college and working for my parents' business. I attend AA meetings at night, but don't say much and try to remain sober one day at a time. After about six months of sobriety my willpower gives out and I relapse. I think about telling my treatment team, my drug specialist, therapist and psychiatrist, all of whom I see weekly, about my drug use but decide against it. Up until this point I have been as honest as I think I can be in my therapy, but pot is a sticking point for them. I want to go back to a four-year school after going to community college and am afraid that if I fess up to my relapse then this will not happen. So, I lie to my treatment team and my family.

I am aimlessly driving around Boston and I start to think about my ordeal with the voices. Some paranoia starts to creep into my consciousness, the kind I felt before the first hospitalization. I go into a gas station to buy some cigarettes. A woman in front of me is arguing with the gas station clerk.

She says, "Why aren't you listening to me! I told you that I am at pump number 6! Why can't I get any service around here!"

I leave the gas station without buying cigarettes. This interaction somehow puts me over the edge and I don't understand why.

I think to myself, "I'd better get out of town before the paranoia gets worse."

I contemplate leaving town until my paranoia blows over. Next thing I know I'm on the highway driving towards New York City. Once I get to Manhattan, I consider calling up my brother and crashing at his place, but the driving bug was still in me. After driving through the night and into the next day I end up in Pittsburg. I call my parents and tell them what happened. My dad gets on a plane to meet me. I get in touch with my psychiatrist and he calls in another prescription to a pharmacy near me. I get on a plane the next day, and my dad drives the car back to Boston. When I get back to Boston, I meet with Dr. Brown. He says that he doesn't want to put me in a hospital since I've had bad experiences there. After consulting with other doctors, he says, "I'm going to put you on Risperdal for a week to give a jolt to your system so that you can reset." I've been on Risperdal before, I didn't like it very much but I agree. I need to reset. I take the drug even though I hate how it makes me feel. I am able to function again after this and I resume my studies. I now have about a years-worth of credits from the college in Florida and about a years-worth from community college.

Throughout this period, a few of my friends stick by me. They aren't happy with my attitude but they remain loyal. Boston is pretty cliquish in general. While in community college there is one clique I hang out with occasionally from High School. Being around people helps me forget about my desire for revenge against the voices and my issues in general, it makes me feel like myself. However, when I'm socializing with most people I feel misunderstood and different. While most of this squad are able to make witty quips and be lighthearted, I resign myself to being on the fringes of the group. One person, named Erin seems to understand my situation a little better than the rest. We end up hanging out more frequently and do our own thing. Erin and I weren't friends from High School, but we became good friends in the years following.

One day Erin and I have dinner at a rib joint. He has previously opened up to me about his traumatic childhood, of going through the mental health system and how difficult that can be. He seems to be offering to help me. In my mind I don't take his offer, but feel like we are closer friends because of his empathetic gesture. I become a fixture at his apartment where he lives with his wife and father.

Ch. 8 The Beast

I am busy during the day, so about once a week I stay up all night and rack my brain for ways to undo the moment that haunts me in my Dad's office. I can't really say much to the voices but I can think of how I reached the point where I was blocked. I can't project myself into "metaphysicality" anymore. I can't move into or away from the voices again. I can't figure out how to do anything pretty much. But I am able to say more to voices when I stay up all night. A few times I convince myself that I have given myself a foothold in solving my issues, but when I go to sleep, the next day everything goes back to the status quo and I'm greeted in the morning to,

"Yeah, that's exactly it."

Although it is less dehumanizing than before, thinking of ways to get myself back rather than a street fight with the voices, it is almost my worst fear. When I was fighting the voices in "metaphysicality" this is what I was afraid would happen, except for the fact that the voices aren't actively attacking me, just constantly interrupting my train of thought saying, "yeah, that's exactly it." There is little for me to work with in terms of what is going on in my mind. I can function, but my mind is pretty much blank. However, I keep coming back to what I was trying to do to the voices while in limbo, to do to them what they did to me, pretty much by any means necessary. In my head I call this the "wrong hard way."

One day, after staying up all night I get some momentum. I am able to speak coherently to the voices only when I stay up all night pretty much, I'm not sure why. All of a sudden, after this all-nighter, I can speak in my head without needing to blink my eye. It is as if my consciousness had reformed in the ether of my cognizance. The first thing I say to the voices with my newfound ability is,

"You haven't made any sense in pretty much five years. The only thing that you have said to me is yeah, that's exactly it. I don't know what you are or why I deserve this, but what you understand and what you believe in is wrong. As a matter of fact, understanding in every sense of the word is wrong when it comes to you."

The voices start getting angry. They say,

"That's how whack he is!?"

I start to explain, "I don't know if you are the same voices as before, but I'm not going out like you want me to. You are going to have to deal with me one way or the other."

They say, "That's how whack he is?!"

I say, "What are you going to do to me that you haven't already done? I'm not afraid of what you can do to me. It's a war of attrition."

The voices say, "That's how whack he is?!"

I say, "Talk is cheap, let's get this started. Bring the raucous!"

The voices start talking inside my head. Not letting me think about anything, annihilating my train of thought.

They say in a booming voice, "You thought you could defeat us but you were defeated, which is why you are like this. You don't really think of anything you're barely hanging on. You don't trust anybody, not even yourself. You can never be like before. We are going to do things to you worse than death."

They go on and on forcing me to follow their train of thought. Their rant lasts a good ten minutes before I'm able to recover. At the end they say,

"You are like us now, you've become everything you hate."

The mendacity of the rant nearly blows my mind. Layers upon layers of lies working together to try to force me to believe something that is false. It is as if they were pounding falsehoods into my brain like a demented drill sergeant. But I fight on, I am myself again to some extent, and I believe in myself. I say,

"Understanding is wrong! Agreeing with you is wrong! You are wrong!"

I think to myself that where I erred before was trying to take on all the voices at once. I adopt a divide and conquer strategy. I decide to try to get some of the voices to agree with me about how understanding is wrong and that agreeing with the other voices is wrong. I go to sleep and the next day I am still able to talk like the previous day. As time goes on it becomes apparent that this is different from before. I wonder if I've moved on from "metaphysically." I begin calling what I was going through, "the beast." "The wrong hard way" becomes a more fully formed idea.

The voices tell me, "You're just doing the wrong hard way! You can't explain it!"

I say, "Yes I can! The wrong hard way is that I change shit in my head to make it normal. You change shit in my head for the sake of changing shit in my head."

Some of the voices agree with me and start to believe in my idea. I do things the way I did when I was in limbo for added affect like,

"The way I second guess myself is the way I laugh and vice versa."

The deceitful rants that try to get me to believe in falsehoods continue.

With my ability to fight the voices back, and now having about two years' worth of college credits, I apply to state school and get in. It is 2013 and I pressure my doctors about my medicine. In my mind, I don't need the anti-psychotic I'm on, my issues before seem long gone and I haven't been hospitalized in about ten years. My doctors finally agree to go along with my plan. Doctor Brown tapers me off the medicine. I keep it cool until I'm almost off the medicine. I am able to compartmentalize my fight with the voices from school and my social life for the most part. Unlike before, the voices seem unable to speak to me when I'm around people. It is only when I am alone that I am struggling with this. My first semester I'm able to take three classes and get good grades. My second semester there I have to drop a few classes. I decide to take summer classes. The voices are ready to take things to the next level. During summer classes is when my life inside my mind begins to boil over into school and my social life.

In school I can't concentrate. I keep on thinking of the "wrong hard way." One of my courses is about the sixties. The discussions in class become hot tempered. Some of the students argue that we should have nuked

Vietnam rather than lose the war and that Malcom X was an incendiary among other hardline positions. "The wrong hard way" appears to be spilling over from my mind into the class. What these right leaning students were saying to the class during discussions seem like something I would say to the voices. Understanding Malcom X's point of view is wrong. Withdrawing from Vietnam was wrong. If you agree with others who don't share this point of view then you are perpetuating an injustice. I didn't believe the shit I was saying to the voices, but I didn't have any other option other than to say shit like that. I was fighting for my life pretty much. What really rankles me isn't just that I disagreed with these arguments, but that I did the "wrong hard way" in the first place because that was what the voices were doing to me. I thought it would fuck up the voices if I used their ideas against them, but didn't really believe in their argument itself.

I begin to question reality again. I stop going to class. I get in my car and drive around, hoping to blow off some steam. The voices in my head ramp up the rhetoric. I drive to Chicago. I calm down a bit and call home. My doctor phones in a prescription for Risperdal to the town I end up in in Indiana. I check into a hotel and take the Risperdal.

Ch. 9 Survival

I sit down and read the journal that I wrote while I was going through my psychotic episodes. It is in a well-worn journal. On the inside cover is the quote, "I am not what I think, I think therefore I am." After the quote reads the statement, "My thesis is: I get to live."

The rest reads as follows: I am the most unstable one in this family because I'm the most stable. Which means I make up excuses that disregard the actual reality. I'm the one that makes the distorted reality maintain. Since I don't acknowledge the problems that we all have, Intermittent clinical depression plagues us. We need to find a way to communicated the incommunicable. I think that my parents don't understand what it means. Like how I was nearly recruited into the military. Because I try to maintain in an introverted way, and the rest of my family doesn't, issues that don't get addressed resonate with unreasonable force when they come to light. Even though I'm prepared to pay for my mistakes I don't want my family to pay for the mistakes I made. I think that we need to have a coping strategy together.

I'm going to write down my thoughts worth saying. My instincts are how I survive. My self-reflection makes me thrive.

Eloquence is more important than style to me, because it takes more character to be eloquent.

Things seem out of place in my thoughts. I'm trying to write down to earth stuff. But the things I write are so concrete they're abstract, so I'm going to flip it. There are good and evil spirits. But the good ones can just as bad things as the evil ones. That's why people who do more than just react to a situation are the wisest. They try to change the situation at the same time. When they do this, they become multi-dimensional. That's why people wo just react are just

caricatures of personalities.

      7.11 I'm telling people at my work that I had food

poisoning when I actually was in a mental hospital for six

days. The reason that I went to the hospital is confusing. I

hadn't been able to sleep for about a week. I was acting very

strangely to my parents this whole time. I wake up late on

Friday morning and threw on some clothing and was trying

to book it out the door so I wouldn't be late for work, but my

parents accosted me. They kept on saying that I needed to

take the medicine, Risperdal and they were furious that I

missed my psychiatrist appointment yesterday. My parents

and I were yelling at each other. My Dad went into his car to

have a cigarette. I went ballistic because they refused to

move their car, preventing me from going to work. I told

them I thought they were trying to make it so I wouldn't get

back into college by getting me fired. One thing led to

another and my parents called the police. I was handcuffed

and brought to the hospital in an ambulance. I was then put into a mental institution and I got out in six days after some hassle. I am now in an outpatient program.

With conversation and dialogue words have more than one meaning. It takes understanding to find the true meaning. Some people choose to understand the way the person is trying to communicate. They can also choose to understand in a different way. I think most of the time people understand in a way that fits them best and that is the essence of a conversation. People go back and forth until they think that they've reached a compromise in understanding. That is the goal of any talented conversationalist. When I put pen to paper I get afraid that I'm being dogmatic. But this is just my perception. I think that wherever I go I vie for the dominant point of view. Even though I desperately try to be humble I'm a righteous individual and I'd fight for the things I care about.

I told a good friend of mine once that I act all the time and that nobody really knows me. It was stupid of me to say that because she was super pissed off at me at the time, but it holds true. I know myself so well that I can literally play any part that I want to. So, I need to learn how to laugh again. I need friends to share a joke with. With nearly all my friends it feels like we're just pretending to be friends and there is so much going on behind the smiling mask we all put on. They all are my friends and they can see behind the smiling mask, but they don't see behind the grimacing one. I think all my friends overcame a lot of personal drama to be in the colleges that they are in and I think this is how we all relate behind the scenes.

Everybody seems to compete with each other over who's the hardest. I'm a realist so I think there is no hardest. Some people are just hard and try not to act that way, which is a poser thing to do. Some assholes just think that the people they deal with are al soft so they brazenly act hard when they're not. And some people act hard at times they need to and soft the times they don't. Some people are just soft. Most people are just plain hard.

It's strange being in a program at the hospital. I've lived near it all my life and heard of people who went here, but I've never been inside its doors. I'm writing some assume things to camouflage my real thoughts, because even though I'm writing in cursive people can still read my handwriting.

I need other people to help clarify my thoughts. Dostoyevsky and other great writers wrote in public places. Writing in public gives a writer perspective. I don't want to write garbage that only I understand. I need other people to be around so I get other contrary input. This helps me write down stuff that is often a compromise between the writer and the reader. Writing in public externalizes internal thoughts. This facilitates free thinking. It takes courage to write in public. It makes me think of the movie 8 mile when Eminem is writing a rap song on the bus. I've got a lot of rhythm and the beat is a lot hotter at a concert then when I bump it in my headphones.

I got a ride to the train by my mother. Waiting in the Amtrak terminal I contemplate why I left Boston on such short notice. I have trouble going to new laces, because I don't like asking for directions and looking like a tourist. It was just on a whim, I had work at the golf course that weekend. I read the Wall Street Journal. I see an advertisement for real estate in Rialto CA and think back to a strange slip of paper I found in my bed as I was packing. It said the name of a restaurant, Rialto, and its address. I was perturbed, since I had never heard of such a restaurant off hand. I decide that I saw the restaurant in VH1's lifestyles of the rich and famous and wrote it down. I'm wearing blue-jeans a Carhart shirt and a baseball cap. The train ride over is uneventful, I pass the time by zoning out. When we arrive at the station I exit the train and see New Yorkers moving like a river. I go with the flow and make my way to the subway. In the subway I need to ask someone for directions, so I buy a People magazine from the newsstand. Tom Cruise and Katie Holmes are on the cover. There is an article in

Rockefeller ✓

there about their upcoming marriage. He gives me good

directions and I hop on the train. I don't sit down in a seat

but stand. A lot of people notice me since I'm 6'3". I get

confused and leave the train way before my stop. I have the

entire day before I meet up with my brother, so I decide that I

might as well walk; accidentally I head south towards

Rocafeller Center. Realizing my error, I turn around a walk-

up Broadway. On Broadway many people offer to sell me

CD's but I only buy two, Ja Fredrick and Logan P. McCoy.

A woman tries to get me to sign up with an environmental

group. Somebody approaches me with a box full of MM's.

He sells me four MM's for ten dollars. Near times square

there is a crowd of people arguing about religion. I walk past

them and realize that I'm walking away from Broadway, so I

walk through the religious soapbox and give the demagogues

a grimace. In Time's Square a homeless person approaches

me and raps into a microphone that isn't connected to

anything. He asks for change but I don't have any. I finally

reach Central Park and there are hundreds of people lounging there sunbathing. I'm parched and hungry because I haven't eaten all day. I haven't sat down since I left the subway. Crossing Central Park, I make my way to museum row. I find a food stand on the corner and buy a sausage and water. Sitting down for the first time in my five-hour long perambulation, my bones creek.

I went into the Guggenheim and studied the paintings. The entire museum consisted of five open floors. My favorite painting was on the second floor. It was a painting of two doves and behind it was a cubist Picasso Painting. I sat in front of it and tried to understand the painting. I walked through every floor, but I was drawn to that painting again. At the bag check they showed a print of an artist who was on 5th St. After leaving the museum I found the artist and he gave me a poster of his print, which I later gave to Andrew. Hearing music in the distance, my feet lead me to a street concert. Part of the street was blocked off. I didn't feel like hanging around, so I took a cab to Union Sq. to meet my brother. My exhaustion succumbed me. I sat down in the middle of the square in the grass. Andrew said he would be late. I was so hungry that I went to McDonald's to have a burger. I meet up with Andrew and we went to Johnny Rockets. We chill out. The rest of my time in NYC was uneventful. We saw Mad Hot Ballroom Dancer, a documentary about kids that are in dancing competitions.

Riding in my green Saber, I look out the window and see a winding hill. I see a fire on top of the hill. People are burning tires and dancing naked around it. I get outside the car and put on my boots. I've been wearing slippers. My destination is Monterey California. This is a detour. Instead of going up the hill I watch from a distance and smoke a cigarette.

The Fires are blazing

The charcoaled food is amazing

Watch the camp fire sputter

Navigating through trees with a rudder

I try to find a place to rest

Where I can feel sleeps caress

I lie down under the tarp

And hope that sleep makes me sharp

On the surface the waves are turbulent. The skipper
of the Song Clipper breathes a sigh of relief, for the wind
blew the vessel away from the coral reef. The ship was
keeling towards starboard. The Song was fat in the water,
for they had been whaling since January in the South Pacific.
In May they would be returning home to Boston and the
crew wouldn't have to go out to sea again for about a year.
But it was dangerous to leave the docks a heavy purse. Some
men hire body guards in advance to escort them home.
However, most of the mercenaries used to be highway men.
Men's hearts don't usually change that easily. The skipper
took over from the pilot away from shore, he knew the waves
better. The pilot suppresses the urge to be insubordinate and
goes below deck.

Noise corrodes my hearing. Loneroid watches the
basketball game with determined focus as though his very

consciousness would affect the outcome of a single shot. The person behind him was perturbed at Longeron's tall stature belches loudly as he shifts positions to get a better view of the court. At the game, the floor seems so much smaller than on TV. At half-time the myriad of noises simmered. The orange koala mascot did summersaults down the stairs of the stadium seating. A man jumped up and yelled "I'm a Eucalyptus tree eat me!"

Loneroid got up to go to the concession stands and the koala's tail smacked him in the face. For good gesture the koala does a summersault on the stairs.

All my lines are congruent

Ending at a point that's altruist

Trying to salvage what's ruined

Picking sides like a druid

When I rhyme with peers

I find welcoming ears

Come to my table and hear leers

Playing softly to seers

Trying to put my head on strait ✓ straight

Thinking to myself heaven can wait

Appetite for rhyming I can't satiate

So, I'm off and running

Words flow like waterfalls tumbling

Thinking versus or just mumbling

At the of a plane thinking of plummeting

When I write I try to be suffice

What's the use of being rich if you can't rock ice

Your unlucky if you run with mice

One line to the next sounds so nice

Each one its own maxim

Each one levying its own tax in income

So, I bang the drum slowly

To most people I seem lowly

Asking people if they want a towel like Towlie

I'm writing words that are absurd

Going to a shaman to get cured

But I can't digest the herb

My feelings are intransigent. I avoid the truth about myself because my mind is befuddled. I think it's because of my medication. I've changed a lot, but my experience in life guides me. I get afraid that my feelings in life are unsubstantiated because if someone in life who is more established comes along with their own feelings about life he could negate mine. Thoughts of isolated thinking spur me on and make me whole. I avoid the truth because I don't want people to know I truly am behind a mask of sociability.

Life is struggling. Writing with desperation I extend who I am. My life is hard. Self-doubt seeps through my confidence. My mind goes from one place to another and I wonder how I got to the place that I am. I like to ponder over who I am and lately I can't. Inconspicuous thoughts creep into my mind and I lose them before I can grab them. So, I think and talk about ideas that re blatant and hope that people understand what I infer about. I need to get back to normal. Ideas disjointedly cloud my cognitive ability. It scares me to make progress because I need it to be in the right direction.

I'm afraid that when I think, it's about a bunch of ideas that I can't really support. But I think I'm on the right track.

I write how the inner self of people dictates their image. If someone is vacuous it is easy to understand that they are transparent; options to someone whose only inner-concern is depleted. For they only react to situations rather than try to mold them into a way of showing the image that they want. That is what I think about.

I feel like I live in my own world at times and a lot of things happen around me. I firmly believe that with discipline I can be put in almost any situation and understand it even if I don't know that led up to that point. I do this by listening very carefully and withhold analysis until later.

Ideas to think about later. When things are confused between groups the best way to deal with it is by explaining the issue exactly, show the groups the point of contention and then find a middle ground through action so the groups will find that there is a productive way to clarify the matter.

So, by showing to groups that they're beefing for the same exact reason they can see that they can work together by having a gray area with the people who know this, so they can reach a common goal even if they're warring with them.

It feels weird to reminisce about going to college. It's been about a year since I've been a college student. Since then I've had two hospitalizations and nearly went to a residential program. The reason why it feels weird is because I've been derailed from my dreams. I want to find a niche for myself.

If the constant situation of life changes every day, how can permanent problems of the world remain salient through the confusion? Humanity is everchanging. Movements occur which change the focal point of reality. That's why the situation of life is everchanging. Groups of people focus on different issues of humanity in order to try and change them for the better or worse. Pain and suffering and also beauty and happiness catalyze the change in focus of the human condition. For most people in the world view success and happiness in a mercantile kind of way. So, they believe that only a limited amount of people can find happiness; which mean as much as people try and be above life's problems (unintelligible) There is always someone on top and someone on the bottom. People make the people on top see the ordeal of the people on the bottom. So, hardships can never be avoided because of the sentience of the struggle always remains for the people who are duped into having to take shit from people on top. To do this in an intelligent way runs society. So, the problems of the world resonate more than the situation.

If people are objective in their point of view anyone can speak truthfully about their perception of the world. But it can't be done alone. It has to be compared to other points of view to be sure that it's on the level of truth, because points of view are built by the facts, which draw conclusions. Every point of view contains truth in it. But it's not the complete truth, because points of view have to mold the truth into a theory. So, while they may list certain facts which explain their point of view, they also have to address facts that prove the opposite. That's why everyone can have an objective point of view because it can be proven or disproven by other POV. *point of view*

The way a person interprets words and actions is the most important part of friendship. I think that it isn't possible for a person to express themselves fully. Part of conversations lack understanding. It is the way that people interpret and see these unspoken concepts that makes friendship work. There are certain things that would be rude to talk about, but should be understood by both parties.

Living in isolation gives me something to write about. But I'm worried that without substance my style will wither. Maybe writing something inconsequential in a big way will unearth the goal of my writing. The small errands in my life have taken over my motivation. Things like doing laundry, seeing my psychiatrist and cleaning my room used to be secondary in terms of my life. School work and smoking weed with my friends were my top priority. Those top priorities were my life, and the inconsequential things supported it. Now, after leaving the residential program, these small tasks run my life. In whatever style I do it in I have to be on point and have initiative. It is my treatment plan to try and build something from my task-oriented life to fulfill my soul.

One ponderous question I have is how do different points of view share the truth? The first thing I need to think about is what points of view are. I think it is perceptions of the truth or how an individual or group interprets the truth. Points of view are the connection of the truth to thoughts and concepts that need to be supported. I think most people don't understand this and get upset by it.

The best way to mediate an argument is to get all the parties involved and to try and forge an agreement. I think that the truth of the matter can be viewed in different ways depending on the points of view. What obfuscates the truth are the intangible connections which facts (unintelligible) I think that is where points of view come into play. Most points of view recognize and apply the facts of the matter but contention comes in on how to make the facts make sense. So, points of view are sometimes vulnerable to disagreement even though they share the same truth. I think the main way to argue against points of views is arguing what you're arguing about. Without this, interlocutors might jeopardize the issues that they agree with in order to argue. This is what I think about when I'm alone.

I think a lot about what defines me. When someone states that I won't be able to go back to school it infuriates me. My mother said straight up that I don't have the mental capacity to go back. It was difficult for me to respond to since I was so galled. I've been going to school my whole life, that is what I've been trained to do. I refuse to believe that the diagnosis of schizophrenia negates all that I've accomplished in going to school.

Society has to have a foundation in order to thrive. The social norms of the middle and upper class are based on the social norms of the lower class (I contend). In the lower class everyone has the opportunity to succeed in life, but they have to show, earn their ticket out of the lower class, because there are limited opportunities. People of the middle and upper classes use political power and money to gravitate towards positions in life. People of the lower class have to carve out lives with perceptions of the truth, because they don't have the money or power to protect their success from people who don't like them. This is the human condition. People have to see the truth when they are poor with every reminder of their low-income living. The upper and middle classes are able to argue about what the truth is in order for individuals to get their way. This is evident with high priced lawyers that allow people to get away with murder. But to me the truth is an irrefutable perception. In order for upper and middle classes to debate the truth, {which they do} the truth has to have a basis, which resides in survival.

Ch. 10 Foundation of Society

I remember showing this journal to my doctor and him using it as a reason not write a recommendation for me to return to college. I can't believe even one word makes sense. The spelling and grammar are pretty good, up until this point, if the handwriting is sort of messy. Images and voices were exploding in my head as I wrote this. I'm still not sure if it makes sense, or it just sort of resonates with me. Regardless, while I was writing this my life was dealing with the fallout of my mental issues on many levels. I don't really remember writing most of it. I haven't read through it in maybe ten years. After this point in the journal it makes less sense and the grammar falls off a bit, but I sort of get what I was driving at, so I'm putting parenthesis to translate. The rest is verbatim.

The most important thing for me in life is to know myself. This takes discipline and hard work. I make daily decisions that seem small, but they define who I am. It is sometimes confusing because I'm not who I think, but I'm whom I make decisions in the position in life I'm in. I have goals and dreams that are inaccessible to me right now, but I'm never going to forget them. As I work to achieve my dreams I'm not the end result of what I want to be. I'm a collection of actions that I make in order to justify the way I think and the way I want to be. People are put in positions, where depending on a person's morals, they have selfless responsibilities. I'm the person defined by the accomplishment and failures of my position.

Acceptance in a group is tantamount in being accepted in life. In groups that have money, they can create their own sense of normalcy. Groups that have money can avoid situations the way poor groups can't, because they have way more options. When you're in a poor group it is impossible to deny pain and suffering, because they see the unfairness of life firsthand. So, their sense of normalcy is situational and reactive to the degradation life throws at them. Much of this would be avoided with money. Anyway, when your accepted in a group and recognize its normalcy, you are taking a big step in understanding the options people have in

182

life, which shows that you understand how life works, individually or in our group, and in other groups {by groups, for the most part that are established in society}

If two people relate to each other in a way that both are ignorant and it's false, is it the same as two people relating to each other with something that's true? For example, if both people mistakenly understand in same way about the mood of a cat. Cat lovers know that cats purr when they're both happy and upset. If both people smile thinking the cat is purring out of affection, then they are both relating to something falsely, if the cat is purring out of dissatisfaction. While the feeling that the people share (smiling at the purring cat) is real, what instigated it isn't. It is my conjecture that awareness about the truth gives a feeling that coincides with the people that people relate to each other. If the cat was purring out of happiness the two people smiling because of this, would have a different feeling than if they were relating to something false

Life is about in-between moments. It is what makes you think, observe and feel actions. Regardless of whether you have to do something, actions don't define us (in terms of what we feel) before and after them (actions).

Why is the context or situation the primary reason for being productive? I think that there are many different ideas on how to make progress in life. But the context is an indicator for moving in the right direction. The goal of being productive is to change the context of things so there's a clear line of what is the correct thing to do and an incorrect thing to do. In most contexts people are saying the same thing in different ways. They argue over what thoughts mean. Compromise means to find an idea that compliment both parties arguments about thoughts. That's why the context or situation is the most important thing about progress.

Everyone tries to connect ideas, in order to express themselves. Ideas at the highest level encompass all other ideas. So (in order to) reach these ideas of the highest level, there has to be a succession of ideas that are better than most. If people don't understand the succession of ideas, (you wouldn't be able to explain the all-encompassing idea)

In most things in life, I just skim the surface. But when something bothers me I try to delve into it to find out why (it bothers me). I don't do this all the time because off the cognitive exhaustion. Also, I have beliefs in life, which I only apply to selective things. The reason being the way my beliefs apply to life. My beliefs justify me not having to expound on them (on the surface level) Because my beliefs justify my actions and I apply (my beliefs) when I have to go underneath the surface (or delve deeper into the meaning of something) to explain why my beliefs seem contradictory when they are not ever.

My feelings are turbulent. Sometimes I feel that I've only just recently grown into myself. I feel that in order to be myself I had to retreat inside myself and put on an act socially with people, because I had difficulties relating.

When I related to people in talking it was confusing because I related to them only in their way, because I think they thought that they knew me better than (I knew myself) In a group everyone compromises on what they are and who I was wasn't compatible with most groups I wanted to hang out with. But I knew who I was as an individual. So, I could relate well with individuals, because I hated the way people (had the tendency to) deny the reality of the world through groups.

I feel as though I explain the obvious. This journal can't be compounded down one bit. I've always wanted to write a novel, but haven't tried before for two reasons. I wanted to get to know women better. And two I have so also much to say. This journal (minus one or two pages) isn't perception it's reality. It is biased and pigheaded but it is more than a depiction of the truth or my life. Everyone has their own truth.

Made in the USA
Lexington, KY
20 September 2019